Mouse and Sunshine
'Til the Break of Dawn

*Mouse and Sunshine
Til the Break of Dawn*

by M.K. Wright

To Krista,
tomatoes 🍅
♡
Mouse

diane

of

tomatoes

to Kiki!

for anyone afraid to say "I love you."

*Mouse and Sunshine
Til the Break of Dawn*

Chapter One

Six months. Six months, exactly.

The date is January 3rd. It is displayed on my phone, and on the departure board to my left. I close my eyes but the digits are still visible. Teasing, burning. Six months. Since the end of us. Since I unlocked the door to my tiny apartment and found the last boy I would ever love half-naked, pressing a girl I'd never met up against the wall, kissing her neck.

I open my eyes, sigh, and shove my phone in my coat pocket. I dust snow off of my coat as I stand in line at the check in counter. I stare out the window as I wait my turn, but all my eyes are met with is a blinding screen of white. The person in front of me leaves, and I step up.

"How can I help you?" asks the worker.

I make myself smile. "Hi, yeah, do you know when the flight to Chicago leaves? I heard it was delayed. I'm just wondering if you can tell me…how delayed it will be, exactly."

"All flights to and from Denver International Airport are delayed until further notice, ma'am," she says.

My forced smile falls off. "How long does 'further notice' go on?" I ask nervously.

"I can't be sure, I'm afraid. But you can go pick up your luggage now, if you like. Sorry for the inconvenience."

"It's um. It's okay. Thanks for the help." I paste another smile on my face (at least I hope it's a smile) and walk to the luggage carrousel, adjusting my bag on my shoulder. There's carols blaring from unseeable speakers, and I mutter under my breath about how Christmas is over, and why don't they change their music already. I'm not usually this cynical, but I guess that's what jetlag does to you.

I finally find the luggage carrousel, and after a rotation or two, I locate my suitcase pull it off with great difficulty. I really shouldn't have packed so many sweaters. I tug it behind me, wandering around with no idea at all where I should go. I end up standing in front of a floor to ceiling window, trying to fix my hair, and smearing on some Chap Stick. I unzip my suitcase and root through it until I find the tiny wooden box I carry my jewelry in when I travel. I've felt half-naked all day without any earrings in, and if I'm going to be here a while I might as well get comfortable.

I pull out a pair of studs my brother gave me as a gift for Christmas a week and a half ago and start putting them in. I have nowhere to set the earring backs until I need to put them in, so I do something my mother used to do when she was short on time or tables, and put the backs between my lips. I've got one earring in and I'm starting on the other when, through the din of the crowded airport, I hear a word called out above all the others.

"Sunshine?"

Which is strange to me because a) There is absolutely no sunshine visible at the moment. The sky, the entire world it seems, is all snow. And b)

Way back in another lifetime, there was a boy who called me Sunshine, because it was almost my name. A boy I had already told myself I would never see again.

"Sunshine, is that you?"

I swear to God that it's his voice. My heart hammers, and my hands shake. I hear my name again, this time closer. A person appears behind me in the window reflection. It's him.

I gasp, and the earring back I was holding between my lips falls down my throat. I choke it down, cursing myself.

"Are you okay?" the boy puts his hand on my shoulder.

I flinch and stare at him through the window. "Mouse…?" I manage hoarsely.

"Sunshine," he says again. His hand drops from my shoulder, and his own shoulders shrug down as he sighs with some sort of satisfaction or something. "Holy…shit. Hi."

"Mouse." I turn around to make sure he's real. In front of me is a tall, three-dimensional person. I called him a boy before, but that's no longer accurate. He has the body of a man. His bone structure is stronger. The curls poking out from underneath his beanie are shiny and soft-looking. There's a pair of headphones around his neck. He's dressed in a thick cardigan with a t-shirt underneath, and worn-in jeans that hug his lean, muscled legs exactly where they should. He wears suede boots on his feet. They look huge.

"Y-yeah. It's me. I can't…you look so…." Mouse gestures at me with one hand vaguely, then drops it down to his leg, and then into his jeans pocket. "Good. You, um, you look good."

"…Thank you." My mind is like a pot left unattended, about to boil over. I can't handle the thousands of thoughts I'm having, so they start spilling over onto the floor.

He steps forward. Either to hug me or shake my hand, I'm not sure, because as soon as he steps forward, I step back. He raises his eyebrows in surprise, but if I had blinked I would have missed it. He recovers quickly.

"Um. How are you?" He scratches his neck.

"What are you doing here?" I ask, ignoring his question.

"What? Oh, I, uh… I was in Wisconsin for Christmas. I'm flying back to Portland. That's where I'm living now. Or I was supposed to be flying back. But I'm told all the flights are delayed."

"Yeah," I say absently. I can't stop looking at him. He's so different. He used to look so fragile. I didn't know someone could change so much in five years.

"So…how are you?" he asks me again.

I look up at him, but only for a moment because it's too hard to meet his eyes. Instead I stare at the wall behind me. "I don't think I'm know how I am right now." I say faintly.

"Oh." His mouth turns down into a little, exaggerated frown, then relaxes into a straight line.

"Yeah." And then there's a beat of silence. That's what they call them in scripts and stuff. Beats. Like a heartbeat. And then there's another beat. And another. Enough to take a pulse with. I really don't want to talk to him. I was fine, or I'd become fine, with never talking to him again. I grip my backless earring in my palm until it could almost pierce my skin. With the other hand, I grab the handle of my suitcase, turn around and walk away from him.

"Sunshine…Wait!" I hear Mouse say as I'm leaving. I grit my teeth and keep walking. If Mouse was any good at hints, he'd just give up and leave me alone.

Only he's not. Mouse was always bad at taking hints, and it was always a problem. Right now, it's sort of a big one.

Mouse has fallen into step with me, and is still trying to make conversation. "So, uh…would you want to go and grab a coffee? Catch up, maybe? There's a Caribou Coffee around here somewhere, according to the directory."

I stop walking and face him. He looks completely serious. How can he be serious? I pinch my whole face together before I sigh and reply, "No, Mouse, I actually don't want to go and grab a coffee right now." I start walking again.

He follows me. "Okay, well maybe we could…"

I cut him off. "I don't want to do anything with you, Mouse." This stops him in his tracks. I stop too, so I can finish talking to him. "I'm tired and pissed and cold and a thousand other things, and I just don't have the patience or the desire to get coffee, or do anything with you. Or anyone. Please just…I have to go."

I start dragging my suitcase behind me again and walk away as quickly as I can without running. I blink away the hurt, confused expression on his face. That face used to melt me. But now it just sort of burns. Mouse's face is seared onto my eyelids and only blinking at the speed of light will flush it out.

(Mouse)

I like flying. I like the thrill and anticipation of liftoff, and I like taking pictures of the clouds dyed pink from the sunrise for my Instagram. I like talking to the stranger who sits next to me. I'm probably in the minority on that one.

The whole experience of traveling by air is just wonderful to me. I become a stranger, everyone else is in their own world and they are all so interesting to watch.

The only downside of it all is jetlag, which falls on me like a ton of bricks as soon as I step off the plane. It's almost as bad as a hangover. It's worse in some ways. At least when I'm hung over I can sleep. But after going home, I don't think I'll be getting drunk again anytime soon.

So when I first see the reflection of my first girlfriend in a window as I enter the terminal, I think that I'm just overtired. After a blink, I expect her to be gone.

Except…she's not.

I think to myself, this must be some messed up déjà vu type shit. But I guess she's always been dreamlike to me.

She looks so different. I mean, it's been like five years, so obviously. Her hair is longer, all the way down her back, when it used to go just past her shoulders. It's frizzing out, and a little flat, so she must have just gotten off a flight herself. It's still beautiful though, her hair—still so dark and curly and shiny.

Her face in her reflection is older, but there's no doubt that it's her. Her cheekbones are sharper, her eyebrows are thick in an Emma Watson sort of way. She's tired, I can tell from the circles under her eyes, the pale undertones in her coffee-and-cream colored skin and the way her shoulders slump, making her whole frame look lopsided and smaller than it already is. She hasn't grown an inch.

I should just keep walking. After everything we were, and what I did to her. I was so young, so stupid. I know that now. The way I ended us was wrong. I shouldn't make her go through everything that would come along with seeing me again.

What would I even say? How would she

react?

I'm about to leave for baggage claim but then I hear myself say her name.

"Sunshine?"

Her reaction was about as good as could be expected. I know I was an idiot, but it still hurt to see her walk away. She's gone. And I am as stupid as I was five years ago.

Chapter Two

I suppose from the start, I was fated to fall for someone just a little bit messed up. I mean, throughout my entire childhood, I had a monstrous crush on Cameron Frye from *Ferris Bueller's Day Off*. My friends always thought that was weird. Mostly because their parents hadn't let them watch *Ferris Bueller* until they were in middle school, and thought that anyone with the last name Frye wasn't worth fawning over.

Mouse isn't much like Cameron, now that I think about it. He's a little too bad-boy to be Cameron. But I don't know; maybe he's changed. It's been four years since we've been face to face; who knows what he's like now.

He does look different, that much I am certain of. His hair used to be a fluffy, curly mop. Now it's shorter, trimmed closer to his head. And his forehead is bigger. Not like his hairline is receding dramatically or anything, but it's definitely bigger. There's even a few creases pressed into the skin there.

And he's taller. Not by very much, though. We were almost the same height back then. I was, and still am 5'6''. He was five foot ten. He's probably around six feet now.

And his jaw. God, if his jaw looked the way it does now, I would have kissed him there all the time.

I should stop thinking of my ex-boyfriend this way. Or at all. I've been so busy thinking about him that now I'm in some part of the airport I haven't seen before. Granted I haven't seen much of it, anyway; I'm usually only here for an hour or two on the days before or after holidays like Thanksgiving and Christmas, and for the most part, I spend that time reading in an uncomfortable plastic chair while I wait to board my flight back home to Chicago.

Now I'm surrounded by cafés and souvenir shops. But I don't want to cart my suitcase through them, so I just sit down on a bench and tip my head all the way back until I'm staring at the ceiling. I sigh and lower my head again.

His face. It was…I don't want to say devastated, because I think that's giving myself too much credit, but he did at the least look a little disappointed. I mean, I would be too, probably. Seeing this person I haven't seen since high school, and asking them to coffee, and then having them interrupt me about how they want nothing to do with me, and watching them stomp away. I'd be disappointed. Probably hurt, too, depending on who it was.

But I'm Mouse's ex-girlfriend. And it wasn't exactly like our breakup was nasty; it was just that long-distance sucked and he didn't think it was worth it. Or something. We were friends for a while after that. We'd email and text. Mouse even brought up the idea of video chat, but I didn't think I could handle it, seeing his face again after all that had been between us, and knowing that all of it was over. Halfway into our senior year, we'd ended it, and by the next summer, I wasn't returning any of his messages. It became too painful. I only agreed to be friends to humor him. And a little bit because I wanted to have some connection to him still. In retrospect, it probably wasn't fair to myself, just jumping back in, pretending everything was fine. I didn't even really get to do the typical breakup thing. The whole Taylor Swift, ice cream, *The Notebook* thing. I tricked myself into thinking everything was okay. I shouldn't have done that. And he shouldn't have asked me to.

    I guess that's why I walked away from him just now. Because he broke up with me, and I didn't really like the reason why. I thought we were gonna make long-distance work. It was only going to last a year. We were planning to go to college together. I thought he had it in him to wait for me; just wait for a year. Our love was something real, something wild and fast. It was love you fight for. Or… so I thought.

    And he asked me to be friends. As if all of the last year had never happened. As if we hadn't been in love. As if I wasn't still in love with him.

I wish we'd both been smart enough to take the time we needed. I wish he hadn't turned all of the lovely thoughts I had of him to dust by treating me, the relationship we'd had like something so easy to transition out of. But none of that happened. And it was such a long time ago, and there is now way to go back and fix it all.

And since this airport isn't taking me anywhere tonight, I may as well stick it out with the only other person I know here.

I get up, and drop my suitcase off again, because God knows I do not want to lug this thing around with me all night long. I keep my coat and my carry-on bag filled with the weird stuff you only ever take to the airport. Things like a neck pillow, (which looks even stupider on me than it does on other people because I have long, thick, curly hair, courtesy of my black father, and when I put it around my neck it's like being strangled.) and my phone charger and three books, because I couldn't decide which I wanted to read, and I could never bring myself to sacrifice the experience of a real book for the convenience an e-reader.

I adjust my bag of airport stuff and go in search of Mouse. After finding a map telling me where the hell I am, I find my way back to where I left him by the window. He's not there of course, so I wander around the space to try and find him. He's nowhere to be seen. I think for a second of getting out my phone and calling him, but obviously I can't do that, because I deleted his number from my contacts the day I stopped speaking to him.

Speaking of speaking, what am I supposed to say to him when (or if) I find him? *Hey sorry for ditching you back there, just been holding a grudge against you for being so insensitive after our breakup. You still up for coffee?*

I probably will end up saying something like that. Only slightly more passive aggressive and vague.

I finally find him in a different section of the airport, leaning on his guitar case, the same one he had when we were together; I can tell from all the stickers on the front. His hands are folded on top and his chin is perched on his hands, as he stares up at the departure board. All the places and airlines are different colors, but they all have the same word at the end: DELAYED.

He yawns and rubs his neck. I throw back my shoulders and walk over to him with purpose.

"Hi again," he says when he sees me. His eyebrows are raised. Understandably.

"Hi. Um. Sorry about back there. It was just…weird. I'd become so used to the idea of never seeing you again. And it was just…"

Mouse fills in for me "It was awkward, because we haven't talked in years, and I kind of acted like there wasn't any sort of tension between us. Because we broke up and all that. Right?"

"That's um…yeah," I reply.

"I'm sorry I did that, Sunshine." He says it sincerely. He never apologizes if he doesn't mean it.

"Thanks. So, uh, about that coffee?"

Mouse smiles and nods, picking up his guitar case by the handle on the side.

Chapter Three

When we were young, Mouse always hated black coffee. He'd either load it up with sugar and cream, or get a blended something or other, a glorified smoothie. But as we approach the barista counter at Caribou Coffee, he orders an Americano.

"What, no peppermint mocha?" I say with a smirk. Around Christmastime, on Thursdays, we'd always walk to the Starbucks a block away from school after we got out of class. He'd order a grande peppermint mocha every time.

"Can't," he says. "I'm diabetic."

"Diabetic?" I repeat.

He nods in affirmation. "Type One."

"Oh. Well. Uh, is...um." I lick my lips. "Are you okay?"

"Yeah," he says with a shrug. "Just gotta prick my finger a few times a day, watch my sugar intake and all that. I'm used to it."

"How long have...?" I start to ask, before the barista clears his throat. We're holding up the line. "Oh sorry. A small peppermint mocha and a...What size do you want?"

"Small's fine."

"And a small Americano. Sorry."

I pay for both our coffees and we sit at a table in front of a tiny fake fireplace with our steaming cups and a strange silence between us. Mouse's posture is still awful, I learn, as he hunches over the table with his drink between his hands. Then I realize I'm doing the same thing, and scoot back in my seat until I'm sitting up straight. After a pull from my festive red cup, I ask him what he does in Portland.

"I work at Powell's, actually." Mouse smiles. He remembers how much I love that place.

"You do?" I can't help but grin.

"Yeah. Just as a cashier, nothing too fancy. And where are you living these days?"

"Chicago." I went to University of Chicago for undergrad, and decided I liked it, so I stayed.

"The Windy City, huh? What do you do there?"

"I'm an intern at Pad & Pen Publishing. Learning the trade."

"So you still want to be an author?"

"I do. I'm working on another book. Or trying to." I say another because I've written two others, one my junior year of high school, and another freshman year of college. Both of the books suck. I'm taking my time with this one. I want it to be at least a little good. Something I'm not embarrassed to talk about. I've only outlined the one I'm working on right now, but I have a good feeling about it. There's just one thing missing. I wish I knew what it was.

"That's good. I'm glad you're still writing.

You were always amazing with words." Mouse says, and bites the lid of his paper coffee cup.

"Thank you, Mouse." I used to write him little poems and throw them at the back of his head in German class. He had a bulletin board filled with crumpled prose written in French. I was only just passing my language course. Mostly because I was so busy writing love notes in French to my boyfriend about his hands that I wasn't paying any attention to the German teacher.

I look at his hands now. He's finally grown into them. They were so big compared to the rest of him when he was 16, hanging from his skinny, gangly arms. His knuckles seem less knobby, and his nails are clean and pink, with little moons taking up half of them. His veins pop out against his skin. I used to like to take his hands and kiss them all over, his knuckles and veins and the tips of his long fingers, and his palms and the inside of his wrists. He was putty in my hands when I did that to him.

It isn't until Mouse moves his hands to his lap that I realize that I have been staring at them. I clear my throat.

"So, are you still doing that music thing?" I ask him.

Mouse shrugs. "Eh. I mean, I do open mic nights sometimes. At coffee shops. I hate doing them at bars. But nothing huge. I'm pretty good at classical guitar playing now."

"Do you still write song snippets on napkins and homework?" He would write anywhere he could when the muse came. On his hands. On mine. And then he would try putting the words together, but they never were quite right. I tried to help him a few times, but then he asked me to stop because he thought all my ideas were better (his words, not mine) and it was discouraging.

"No, I haven't. Not since…" Mouse sighs and shifts in his chair. "I mostly do covers. I play around with arrangements of my favorite songs. Maybe I'll try composing sometime." "I really liked the lyrics you'd come up with."

"No," Mouse laughed humbly. "They were terrible. They were so bad."

"They were only a little bit bad." I smile.

He smiles back. The thing about Mouse is that he smiles very selectively. He's got this ghost, this wisp of a smirk on his face almost all the time, but it's hard to make him actually smile. But when he does, it's like his face breaks open, and the sun is shining out of the cracks at you. And it almost hurts you, but you can't help but keep looking, and you feel warmer and happy, and you'd do anything to keep him smiling like that forever. I'd always called it his blue-ribbon smile, because if there was ever a contest for the best smile, he would win it. Always. Hands down.

"Are you still doing YouTube?" Mouse swills his cup around by its base.

"Hmm, yeah. Not as much though. And it's mostly about books. It's all about books. I'm a BookTuber."

"That's interesting. What exactly does a BookTuber do?"

"Well, I read and review books. There are liveshows where viewers and vloggers talk about books together. There are book tags. Like 'pick your favorite character' or whatever." I stop talking and consider my explanation for a moment. "It sounds dumb, doesn't it?"

"No. No, no, it doesn't. BookTube. It's very you, Sunshine. I bet you're a great critic."

I shrug and slouch into my seat. I'm too tired to have good posture. "I'm okay. It's just a hobby, really. I don't do it nearly enough to appease my subscribers. How's your coffee?"

Mouse looks down at his cup. "Good, I think. I haven't been paying much attention to the flavor. I was distracted by you." He takes a sip of it.

"Well."

"What? Do you not like it?"

"No, I mean it's fine. I just wish I'd ordered something I actually liked."

"Why didn't you?"

"Distracted. By you." His face becomes splotchy.

"What would you have ordered if you weren't distracted by me?"

"I've become something of a tea aficionado."

"Interesting."

"Do you drink it?"

"No. I hate tea."

Mouse sighs and shakes his head. "Unbelievable."

I roll my eyes and stretch. "What time is it, do you know?"

Mouse checks the watch he wears on his left wrist. "Four fifty-six," he reports.

"Do you think the flights are back online yet?" I ask.

"I doubt it," Mouse says, scratching his stubble. Stubble. Another new thing.

"Yeah, you're probably right. Ugh. What are we supposed to do for until 'further notice'?"

"What?"

"I mean, we could be here for hours. Probably even overnight. Do you know how boring that's going to be? Especially after all of the stores close down for the night." I start to panic. The only sustenance I have is a smushed muffin from the Starbucks at the Spokane International Airport. I'm gonna starve to death.

"You're not gonna starve to death," Mouse says. It would appear that I said that last bit aloud. "The shops don't close for a long time. Also: vending machines."

"Yes, there is nothing I love more than White Cheddar Cheez-Its that are three months past their expiration date."

"I see your love of sarcasm has not faltered," Mouse remarks.

I let a smirk crawl onto my face. "I'll still be bored. I guess I'll just read all night."

"You're just…gonna read?" Mouse echoes.

"Yeah. I mean, what else would I do?"

"I mean. I um. I just, if you want, we could hang out. Like old times. Uh, except not. Because….what I mean is we could keep each other company. Wander around. I've got my laptop; we can watch movies. Whatever. You don't have to. I mean, if you'd rather read."

I take a sip from the cup filled with Americano. Mouse raises both his eyebrows at me.

"Sure," I say. "Yeah, we can hang out. It'll be fun."

"Yeah?" Mouse perks up. That smile needs to stop being on his face immediately.

"You're way too excited about this."

"Excuse me for being happy to spend the day with someone I haven't seen for years."

I sigh fondly, and stand up. I toss the cups in the trash. "We doing this?"

"Fuck yeah, we are. Mouse and Sunshine 'til the break of dawn." He hops out of his chair. I shake my head at him. "Or however long it takes for us to get out of this purgatory."

"Come on then, modest Mouse."

Mouse follows me out of the coffee shop, and out into the mulling crowds.

Chapter Four

It's fun at first. We stroll through flower and souvenir shops, spend way too much time in a candy store, and wander around and around, not caring if we get lost, because we've got hours to find out where we need to be.

"So, tell me about life in Portlandia," I request in the bookstore.

"I live in an apartment near the uptown shopping district with two other guys. They're about as accomplished as I am."

"What's that mean?" I ask, reshelving a cookbook I'd picked up.

"They're still trying to figure shit out." He opens a book to a random page. "Like me."

"Oh. Do you have a car?"

He puts the book back. "Nah, I bike everywhere. I live pretty close to work and everything else I need. Biking is kind of the ideal form of transportation in Portland. Being green and all that."

He walks past me to the fiction section. The constant bike riding is evident in the muscles of his legs, and the godlike perfection of his ass.

I very much need to stop checking out my ex-boyfriend. Especially this early into the evening. Just especially.

Right now, we're in the airport's little bookstore, which reminds me entirely too much of the way I met Mouse.

As one may have gathered at this point, I have a slight thing about books. I lived close enough to the mall during high school that I would go there to study every day after school. There were a couple girls from my sixth period History class that would sometimes invite me to their houses after school, but I always turned them down. I wanted them to be my History friends. Taking it out of the classroom was going to make it weird. Anyway, I never would see them again after graduation, so what was the point? I hate goodbyes.

On a Wednesday in mid-September, as I was sitting at a small, circular table covered with my Chemistry notes, I saw a boy wandering between the shelves.

Which wasn't uncommon. But this boy? He was skinny and bow-legged, with a pile of light brown curls on his head, and clear, blue eyes. His skin was pasty and his posture was atrocious. But something about him made me just want to look at him, and not stop looking. He looked sad. Not overtly, more like he tried to hide it. Like the sadness lived under his skin. Making his big blue eyes tired, and his mouth a simple pink thing, and his eyebrows rest heavily over his lids.

I saw this boy between the shelves, picking up a book and flipping it open, or flipping it over, and reading the synopsis. He mouthed the words to himself, and once I watched his lips move for the entire time it took for him to read the back of a softcover.

He was looking for a book, but didn't seem to be having much luck finding one he was interested in. I've been called an expert in the business of making book recommendations, and I knew that after asking him a few simple questions, I could pull a book that he was sure to like.

The only problem was that I was horrible at introductions. So for a good twenty minutes, I watched him browse books from my table at the adjoined Starbucks. He caught me looking at him once. I pretended there was something in my eye.

In the end, it was Mouse who talked to me first. I'd plucked up the courage to at least search through the same aisle as him, and he was only five feet away.

"Do you know if this is any good?" he asked, holding up a copy of *Great Expectations*.

"It's classic. I mean, I haven't read it myself. It's not really my genre."

"Yeah," he said, replacing it on its shelf.

"What do you mean, it's not your genre?"

"Well, most people have a book genre they gravitate towards. Like…mine is Young Adult."

"Any Young Adult?"

"Any and all."

"But not classics?"

"Not…often. Only if they're for a class or something. I usually only read classics for fun if they're YA classics. Like, I love *Catcher in the Rye*."

"Yeah? So do I."

"What other books have you read?"

"Lately? Hmm. A couple weeks ago, I read *Perks*. I really…Chbosky really got to me, y'know?"

I nodded. "That book is amazing. Um, out of curiosity, what sort of music do you listen to?"

"The Mountain Goats are my favorite. Also Elliot Smith, and Black Sabbath. And Modest Mouse. All that weird shit."

I blinked in surprise at his language. Not that I minded, but most people don't start swearing after only knowing someone for a minute.

"What?" he asked, evidently unaware he had said something some people might find offensive. "Oh, sorry, I said 'shit' didn't I? God, I said it again. I'm such a shit head. I mean…! Sorry. Sorry."

"It's fine. You could have said 'fuck' and then we would have been in real trouble."

He raised his eyebrows. "Are you quoting *Love Actually* at me?"

"Maybe I am." I smile I smile and shake my head. "So, kind of an indie type of guy." "I guess?" He kneaded the flesh at the back of his neck. "I don't know. I just want to read something."

"I think I can help you with that. Let's go

to the YA section. I don't think you'll find what you're looking for over here."

"Okay. Thanks. Um, I'm Abbot, by the way," he said as he followed me.

"Mm, Abbot Mortimer?"

He smiles faintly and shakes his head. "Abbot Jennings. Most people jump to Abbott and Costello. But Abbot Mortimer, the mouse from *Redwall*? That's who my mom named me after."

"I loved *Redwall* as a kid. My dad would read them to me before bed."

"My mom would do the same thing."

"It's a pleasure, Abbot Jennings."

"Call me Mouse. Everyone does. Everyone who really knows me."

"I only just met you. How can I *really know* you already?" Though the idea was completely welcomed by me.

"If you work here, I have a feeling I'll be

seeing you a lot. What was your name? I haven't asked yet, have I?"

"I don't work here. But my name is Soleil."

"So-lay?" Mouse repeats. "As in, French for the sun?"

"Yeah. My dad is from France. But most people can't pronounce Soleil so everyone just says 'Sunshine' instead. Call me Sunshine Ballanger."

"*So-lay Bell-on-jay*. That's the most French French name I've ever heard. What's your middle name?"

"Amelia. It's German, though."

"Oh."

"…What's your middle name?"

"Wilson. I don't know where it came from. Besides my grandfather."

"Was your grandfather by any chance a

volleyball?"

Mouse blinked slowly at me and shook his head microscopically, a hint of a smile on his face.

"So tell me, Sunshine," Mouse said as we reached the YA stacks. "How do you know so much about books but not work at a bookstore?"

I snorted. "I don't know that much about books. And I don't know. I would apply if they were hiring." I scanned the shelves for the John Green books.

"They are hiring," Mouse said. "Didn't you see the sign?"

"You're a funny guy, Mouse. If Barnes and Noble was hiring, I would know about it."

"What are you looking for?" Mouse asked me.

I was on my hands and knees, studying the spines of all the books on the bottom shelf.

"John Green. Do you see John Green?

He's usually right here."

"The John Green books are up here."

"What? No." I stood up. Mouse pointed at the shelf to his right. And sure enough, several copies of John Green's books march across the shelf in color coded blocks. "Oh. Well, I'm really great at paying attention to things today." I slide a copy of *Looking for Alaska* from the shelf. "Here. Read this. It's his first novel; not as good as *An Abundance of Katherines* but it's up your alley, I think. It's a coming-of-age novel written from a guy's perspective."

"Is that my genre?" Mouse asked, taking the book from my hands and reading the description on the back.

"Coming-of-age? I think that it could be. I mean, I'm sort of winging it, but I've been told I'm pretty spot-on with this sort of thing."

"It's all right. I trust you. I bet it's great. I mean, it's got this shiny sticker on it that says what? Printz Honor Award. Sounds fancy." The corners of Mouse's mouth turned down in a sort of 'Huh, impressive' expression.

"It's a kind of prestigious award, I think."

"Prestigious awards *and* the Sunshine Ballanger seal of approval. I guess I have to read it now."

"Guess so. Oh, wait, let me see that." I took the book from his hands and went back to the table where my neglected homework sat. I ripped the corner off of one of my pieces of notebook paper. I scribbled my cell phone number on it in purple ink, and stuck the scrap of paper between the pages of the book.

"What did you do to my book?" Mouse asked, taking it back as I held it out to him.

"Read it, and you'll find out." I smiled at him.

Mouse smiled back, and that was the first time his smile hit me fill force. His eyes crinkled and his eyebrows caved in on each other. Mouse smiled with every muscle of his face. I literally had to sit down.

"Well, um, it looks like you've got some homework to get cracking on. So I'll stop bothering you now. It was really swell to meet you Sunshine. Have a great day."

"You too," I replied, my voice cracking. I hoped he didn't notice.

He flashed a tiny grin at me before he walked off to the checkout. I watched him until he left the store and I couldn't see him from my spot anymore.

I finished my homework, and got an application for the cashier job they were hiring for. I returned it the next day. I got a call that night, saying I got the job. I was there all the time, anyway, they said; I might as well start getting paid for it.

Presently, it's five seventeen, and we are sitting on a bench in a quieter part of the airport, sharing a bag of tortilla chips.

"So where did you end up going to college?" I ask, licking the salty dust from my fingers.

"I went New York University. It was amazing. I mean, I was totally broke. But it was so much fun."

"What made you decide to move across the country after school?"

"I heard about their doughnuts." I raise my eyebrows. Mouse laughs. "I wanted to live in another city in the Inland Northwest. Portland just seemed up my alley."

"What did you study at NYU?"

"Well, I thought about a music major, but my dad said it was a waste of time, so I settled for English. Which I liked a lot. But then the whole being broke thing made me realize that I don't have enough talent or ambition to do anything in a career that having an English degree gets you. I mean, besides teaching. But I didn't really want to do that. So I switched to Engineering, in hopes that I'd be able to get a better paying job in less time."

"But you're working at a giant bookstore," I state.

"Yeah. Yeah, I am." Mouse pulls a folded over chip from the bag.

"That's…not that profitable of a career, I assume."

"No, it isn't. But I'd rather be working a job in an environment that I like while I try to figure out a career that I like and is also well paying. I decided that being an engineer would be the most boring thing in the world after I graduated." Mouse pops the chip in his mouth.

"Talk about a waste of four years," I say.

"Only two and a half. I was an English major first. That was fun. I wrote a bunch of short stories. And I guess they didn't suck too much. I got a high B in Creative Writing."

"Not too shabby, Jennings."

"I bet you got an A, though, didn't you?"

"Every semester," I admit.

"That's what I thought."

"Oh, hush." I shove his arm and take the bag of chips from him.

"So, you said you went to Chicago for college?"

I nod. "University of. For English, obviously. With a creative writing concentration. Again, obviously. I got an internship at Pad & Pen Publishing my senior year, and I've been there for about a year now. It pays pretty well, considering. There are three other interns I work with on a daily basis. They're…something."

"Something?"

"I don't know, like weirdly competitive. With office stuff. Sucking up to the bosses, trying to out-do each other. It's stupid. But it's also pretty entertaining to watch."

"Do you live with roommates?"

"No, I've got a tiny studio apartment in the super sketchy West side of Chicago. But I haven't been mugged yet."

"Congratulations. Wear that badge with pride."

"Oh, I do. Only not too much, because then somebody might just feel inclined to mug me and revoke it."

"Oh, of course. Silly me."

"Yeah, seriously, Mouse, what were you thinking?" I laugh.

Mouse shakes his head and chuckles. "Not much, Sunshine. I don't think enough. I thought you knew that."

"I guess I sort of forgot. Cut me some slack, I haven't seen you since I was seventeen."

"Alright, alright."

"Thanks," I say, and sit back on the bench.

Mouse leans back, too, facing me. His

eyes are looking at mine, so I look right back. Mouse's eyes used to be clouded over. Metaphorically speaking, I mean, for the most part. But you could always tell that his mind was elsewhere. But now his eyes are clearer. Brighter, and definitely happier. He looks like he's all there. He looks alive, and awake. He's fresh and present. He used to bounce his leg with anxiousness and agitation, but now his foot taps to the Christmas music (that should have stopped playing days ago!).

    Mouse got better while he was gone from me. And I don't know if this fact makes me happy or sad.

Chapter Five

Now it's six o' clock and we're in a different part of the airport, eating really good bagels from Einstein Bros., and reading. Just like I would have done if I was by myself. But it's Mouse next to me now, our legs kind of criss-crossing together. I'm rereading a paperback that I've had for years, and practically have memorized. It's just as good as the first time.

I put my book in my lap and lift my arms over my head and stretch. My eyes open, and fall on Mouse's book. The paperback is battered and dog eared. The cover is black, with a single purple candle on the front.

"Is that…" I start.

"The copy of *Looking for Alaska* you gave me when we met? Yeah." He looks up from the book and beams at me.

"It's *dead*, Mouse."

"No, it isn't. It's completely readable." He

flashes the pages at me. "See?"

"It's all scribbled and highlighted and all the pages are turned down."

Mouse starts reading the book again. "Not all the pages. Just the ones with the best words."

"Why don't you buy a new copy? That one's a mess. How are you even reading it?"

"My eyes are surprisingly good for reading." He flips a page.

"But there's so much writing in the margins. So much between the lines."

"I like it. It's personalized. I love this book. It's special."

I want to ask what makes it so special. But I'm afraid of the answer. I ask anyway.

"…Why?"

Mouse stares at me. "What did you say?"

"Why is it so…special?"

He flicks the pages back, and holds it open for me to see. "It's signed."

"Oh." Thank God.

"Yeah. John Green came to Powell's once. It was amazing. I got to talk to him a little bit."

I sit up and close my book. I lean forward. I need to hear this story. "You did? What did you say?"

"I said *Looking for Alaska* was the best book I've ever read."

I bite my thumbnail. "And what did he say?"

"He said, 'I think it's the worst book I've written. Well. Worst finished book.'"

"And what did you say then?"

"Well, I asked him why."

"Yeah?"

"Yeah. And he said, 'The first one is

always the worst one. Not like I'm not proud of it, but, like, it's not good.'"

"Are those his exact words?"

"Yes. I memorized them. He also suggested that maybe it wasn't the best one I've read, but my favorite. He was right, of course. And then I asked him to sign the book, and that was it."

"I am thoroughly jealous."

"As well you should be."

Mouse finished reading *Looking for Alaska* two days after I gave it to him, and he called me that Friday. I was knitting by the fireplace in my dad's big squashy armchair. Only he was allowed to sit in it, but he caught me once and said as long as I didn't tell my brother, I could keep sitting in it. When I got a call from an unknown number. I took the call and cradled my phone between my ear and shoulder while I continued knitting.

"This is Sunshine."

"How could you do this to me," said a voice I hadn't yet recognized.

"Um, I think you have the wrong number, sir."

"Is this Sunshine Ballanger?"

"Uh, yes…"

"Sunshine, this is Mouse Jennings. We met the other day at Barnes and Noble. You gave me a copy of *Looking for Alaska* by John Green, and it has simultaneously ruined and changed my life."

"Oh, Mouse. Hi." I could feel my smile on my voice and hear it in my voice.

"Don't you 'hi' me, little Miss Sunshine."

"Oh, good one. Never got that before," I deadpanned.

"Stop evading me. You have presented me with the most important book I have ever read."

I set down my knitting needles and pulled my legs up to my chest.

"What makes it so important? Because often people misread it." If he misread it, that meant he was different from the person I thought he was, which would potentially ruin everything.

"I mean, it just made me really understand the toxicity of holding a girl on such a high pedestal. It's so dangerous to treat them like some sort of...fairy princess. Or..."

"Manic pixie dream girl?"

"Yes! Yes, that. Exactly. I mean, Pudge loved her, but for all the wrong reasons. And he didn't understand how fucked up she was until it was too late."

"Oh, yes, you get it. I'm so glad you get it."

"I'm so glad we're on the same page. Hey, the same page. Ha."

"Ha," I said back.

"So, Sunshine."

"Mouse."

"I would like nothing more than discussing this fine piece of literature in person."

I smile and sit back in my chair. "Is that the truth?"

"Yeah. Would that be cool with you?"

"Um…" I rumpled the hair at the back of my head. "Sure." That was an understatement. I had been thinking about him all week.

"Really? Awesome. I was a little worried you'd think I was a freak or something."

"I wouldn't think that."

"No? Really? Thanks."

"Do a lot of people think that?"

"I don't know. Probably. I don't really have any friends at school."

"Which school do you go to?"

"Shadle."

"Really?"

"Yeah, where do you go?"

"I go to Shadle, too."

"No way, really? What year are you?"

"Junior. What about you?"

"I'm a junior, too. How have we never seen each other?"

"Maybe you have seen me," I suggested.

"No. No, if I'd seen you, I would remember. You've... got one of those faces."

"It's the hair, isn't it?" My hair is my most defining characteristic. It's all the way down my back (but back then it was a little past my shoulders), and people always want to touch it. I don't brush it; I only yank a pick through it every few days, right after I wash it. It's bushy and untamable, so I just let it fall down my back and shoulders.

"Oh, it's totally the hair," Mouse laughed. "What lunch period do you have?"

"Second. What about you?"

"I have first. And I ride the bus to school and back home."

"And I hate the bus, so I walk."

"Ah, see, this is why we never see each other."

"I guess so. But hey, guess what?"

"What?"

"You have a new friend."

"I do?"

"Duh: Me."

"Right, yes."

"You do want to be friends, right?"

"That would be kind of amazing."

"Only kind of?" I teased him.

"I'm keeping my expectations low," he laughed.

"Not necessary, but okay. So, you still wanna talk about this life changing book?"

"Ah. Yes. But not at school. Maybe a coffee date? After school?"

"A coffee *date*?" I wanted to make sure I wasn't setting myself up for embarrassment.

"Yes, I said date. Why? Do you just want to be friends? Am I being too forward? I can never tell if I'm making people uncomfortable. That's probably why I haven't succeeded in the friend-making business."

"No. Yeah. I mean, yes. A date. For coffee. That sounds good. It'll be fun." These were the only intelligent words I could form.

"Really? Awesome. Is tomorrow okay?"

"Tomorrow is great."

"Cool beans."

"Cool beans."

"Well, I have a US History chapter to not read, so I'm going to stop bugging you know and let you get on with your life. Have a good night, Sunshine."

"You too, Mouse. See you tomorrow."

"Yeah." I could hear his face-breaking smile through the phone receiver, and it tied my stomach up in knots. "Tomorrow."

Chapter Six

It's 7:00 and we're standing at a phone charging kiosk. Mouse is scrolling through Twitter, while I flick through my Facebook feed.

"So," I say, not looking up from my phone. "I see you've got Kelly Sue with you."

"Mm? Oh." Mouse pulls his focus from Twitter and looks at the ground, where his guitar case, containing the instrument he has named Kelly Sue, rests between his legs. "Yeah. She looked lonely. I decided to let her come with me."

"That was nice of you."

"That's what Kelly said."

I laugh at that. Part of Mouse's charm was how he treated his guitar. He's had it for longer than I know, and he takes such good care of it. He acts as if it's a living thing. Sometimes I think he thinks she really is.

"What's the last thing you learned?"

"I taught myself 'In the Aeroplane Over the Sea' last month."

"Really? I love that song."

"Do you want to hear it?"

"Um, duh."

"Okay. Come on, let's sit by the wall." Mouse picks up his guitar and walked the few steps to the wall, and finds an empty spot where we won't bother anybody too much. We slide down to a seat, and Mouse unbuckles his guitar case and pulls Kelly Sue out. She's just as beautiful as I remember.

"I'm gonna play without a pick. It's quieter that way. Which means fewer people will glare at us."

"That's probably a good idea, then."

"Yeah." Mouse settles Kelly Sue in his lap, and after positioning his fingers on the frets, he starts strumming.

He sings softly with a slight twang and a

lilt in his voice. His singing voice is deeper than it was before. We used to do talent shows in school and sing songs together when we were bored. His singing was never failed to make me smile. And my voiced harmonized so nicely with his.

His singing now is braver, somehow. More daring. He even changes some of the notes, making them higher or lower in surprising but not unfitting places. He even whistles in the middle.

And when he's done, I start to say, "That was really good", but my voice is drowned out by clapping. We look up to see a small gathering of people around us, who have apparently been watching Mouse sing. Neither of us have noticed.

Mouse's neck gets splotchy and he manages to flash an almost-smile before bowing his head bashfully.

I nudge his arm. "They like you. Play something else."

He looks at me. "Really?"

I nod vigorously.

He thinks for a moment. "Okay. But will you sing with me?"

"Eh, why not. What have I got to lose?"

"Okay. 'Lazy Confessions'. Like we used to do. Remember?"

I smile fondly. "Yeah, I do."

Mouse plucks the chords, and starts to sing. He starts the lines, and I finish them, and we sing the choruses together. It's a quirky little song by the Moldy Peaches, and features slightly nonsensical, stream-of-consciousness lyrics. But it's cute and fun, and easy to remember, so we sing it, grinning the whole time.

There's more clapping, and a few more people have decided to watch us tired young people sing silly old songs. And we couldn't possibly let them down now, could we?

"Now what?" Mouse whispers to me.

"What other songs have you got in your arsenal?"

"Music isn't a weapon, Sunshine."

"That's not what I meant, and you know it." I roll my eyes. "Just think of another song. Something less underground this time."

"Hmm," Mouse plinks the minor strings thoughtfully. "Oh, I know. 'Dog Days Are Over'. You take most of it, but I'll do the choruses with you."

"You want me to sing Florence + The Machine solo?"

"Florence is a solo artist. So yeah. You can do it. You sing her well. Come on, Sunshine, give the audience what they want." He says this like the joke that it is.

I squirm into a better sitting position. "Fine."

Mouse starts plucking. My heart beats crazily, and I look at anything but the small crowd.

I sing and clap where the drum beats

would be. The crowd starts clapping, too, and suddenly singing gets easier.

I'm just starting to enjoy myself, when a security guard decked out in black forces his way through the small crowd.

"You can't busk in an airport," he says firmly.

"We're not busking. We're just singing. These people came of nowhere," Mouse says.

The security guard looks down at our feet. Probably for a hat or something for people to drop money in. Mouse's guitar case is closed.

"Open your case, sir," he demands.

Mouse tosses the lid back. It's empty, of course.

"Hmm." The guard turns to face the people. "All right, every one, break it up. The show's over."

The crowd disperses. He turns back to us.

"Move along." He walks away.

Mouse blows a puff of air from his lungs. "Well, that was fun while it lasted."

"Yeah." I stand up, and offer him my hand. "Come on, let's go get Ben & Jerry's. They've got sugar-free something, right?"

Mouse puts Kelly Sue away, and takes my hand. I pull him to his feet and we start walking.

Chapter Seven

The day after our phone call, Mouse and I walked to the Starbucks a few blocks away from school. We talked about the book the entire way there, and until his coffee had gone cold, because he had too much to say to drink it, and until mine was all gone, because all I could do was listen and nod.

Mouse really understood the book. I leaned over the table, holding to every word he said, nodding and nodding, and when he paused for breath, I would say, "Yes. *Yes*." Because he was so right and perfect I couldn't say anything else that he hadn't already said. Also because his voice was wonderful to listen to.

There was one lull in the conversation, and it was forty five minutes into our date.

"Oh God, I've been talking this entire time, haven't I? I'm sorry. I'm such a shitty date," Mouse said during it.

"Oh, no, I don't mind at all." I lifted my

cup to drink, but of course there was nothing left to drink, so I set it back down.

"No, but seriously. Talk. Tell me about you. I'm curious. I really am." Mouse sipped his green tea Frappucino.

"Well… growing up, I spent all of my summers in France. My dad's family lives in the country, near Paris, so I know that city like the back of my hand. It's gorgeous. My father and I used to skip rocks in the Seine. And I speak fluent French."

"You do? No way."

"Yeah, way."

"Say something."

"Hmm…" I sat up straight; I had been slouching over the table, I guess sort of subconsciously trying to be closer to him. "Okay. *Je vous aime un peu plus que je ne devrais, je pense. Mais votre voix est comme une chanson, et je ne peux pas arrêter de regarder vous.*"

"What did you say?" Mouse asked.

"Hmm, I don't know if I'll tell you."

"Aw, why not? It sounded so cool."

"Because the translation…it'll sound weird."

"I don't care."

"I'll paraphrase."

"No, give me the direct translation." Mouse kicked me under the table and grinned. "Please?"

He could make me do anything with that smile. I spouted the words right out. "I love you a little more than I should, I think. But your voice is like a song, and I cannot stop looking at you."

That was when I learned that Mouse's neck got splotchy when he was embarrassed.

"See, I told you it was weird." I shook my head, and hung it, letting my hair fall down to hide my face.

"No," Mouse said quietly. "No, it isn't weird."

"I said that I love you, Mouse. I've known you for three days."

"Is it not true?"

"Well, it's a little too soon to love you, isn't it?"

Mouse laughed. "Yes, maybe a little."

"It was the closest word to 'like' that would be correct in context. I'm not in love with you, Mouse."

"Aw, you're not?" He pretended to pout.

"No, not yet," I said. And then, because I was feeling weirdly brave, "Give it time."

Mouse's eyebrows turned up sweetly. And I thought to myself that it might not take that much time to fall in love with him at all.

Airports are so boring. Nobody was ever meant to be in them this long, with no escape.

We're back to browsing the tiny shops. I'm checking out a shelf of Denver, CO snow globes.

"Hey," Mouse says. "What do you think of this?"

I turn around to find Mouse in head-to-toe Broncos merchandise. He has a foam finger on each hand, three different hats, and is wearing countless lanyards around his neck.

"Take all of it off immediately."

It's not me who says this, but the cashier behind him.

"Unless you're planning to buy all of that stuff."

Mouse makes a guilty face, and starts putting everything back where it belongs.

"Every employee in this airport is such a party pooper," he murmurs to me, as I take the lanyards off his neck. "Like, is fun even a thing in

Denver?"

"It's hard to tell," I reply, patting down his hat hair. "I've only had the chance to meet the pleasant folk who keep this airport running."

"Yeah, me too. We should probably leave now."

"Good idea."

We leave the souvenir shop and lean against the wall outside of it. I take my glasses off my face and wipe them on them with the hem of my shirt.

"Now what?" Mouse asks.

I shrug and start walking around aimlessly. Mouse trails behind me.

Then it occurs to me. "Oh!"

"What?" Mouse asks.

"This place has a bar, right?" I say, as I turn back around.

"Um… Yeah. Somewhere." Mouse doesn't sound too interested.

"Let's go find it!" I scramble off to find a map.

"Really? That's what you wanna do?" Mouse follows after me, his hands swinging in the pockets of his cardigan.

"Yeah! Doesn't that sound better than standing around and looking at departure boards that aren't going to budge anytime soon?"

"Erm…I don't know. I guess."

"Come on Mouse, where's your enthusiasm?"

"I don't really have any when it comes to drinking."

I stop talking and turn back around. "You don't drink?"

"Not really. At all. Ever. Anymore."

"Exactly why not?"

Mouse shrugs his shoulders. "But if you want to go, we can. I'll just watch you get wasted. It should be interesting."

There's something this boy isn't telling me.

"Are you sure? We don't have to go if it's not an environment you're into. There's other stuff we can do. I mean, there's more stores. Or we could read. Or…we'll think of something. We don't need alcohol to have a good time."

"You sound like a D.A.R.E. sheriff or something."

I sigh. "I know. Why don't you drink anymore, Mouse?"

"I guess the results of Drug Abuse Resistance Education just kicked in a little late." The corners of his lips twitched wryly.

"Stop it."

"Hmm? Stop what?"

"You're avoiding my question." I fold

my arms.

"You're right." Mouse walks past me to the airport directory. "I am."

"But why?"

"Look, do you wanna go to the bar or not? Because I'll go with you. We can still talk." Mouse says with mild exasperation.

I feel smaller as I say, "No. It's fine. Let's just…" I sit down on the nearest bench, and take the book I was reading earlier from my bag and open it.

After a few moments, Mouse sits down next to me with *Looking for Alaska*. We sit in silence, flipping pages, with an obvious tension between us. After about half an hour, it's been long enough that the tension is mostly diffused. To extinguish the rest of it, I sit sideways on the bench, brining my knees up to my chest, and leaning my back against Mouse's arm.

I turn the page and start a new chapter.

"I'm sorry for snapping," he says. "It's just…"

I lower my book to listen to him.

"When I came home for Christmas, I learned that my dad had started drinking a lot more. Mom said it started when Gloria told them she was gay. Now he hardly talks to her and he was sort of wasted all week, and I already kinda hate him, so now I just have another thing that I can't do without thinking about him."

This is heavier than I had expected. "Mouse, I'm so sorry."

"It's alright. Beer tastes like piss anyway," he says bitterly.

We both go back to reading. I reach behind myself for his hand, and grasp it in mine. I pull his arm around so it rests on my right shoulder, and I twist my head to kiss the spot on his hand where his thumb and the back of his hand meet. I squeeze his hand and let of it. He puts his hand on my shoulder and rubs it.

"Thank you for understanding, Sunshine."

"It's all I can do, Mouse."

"I know. But it's so…thank you."

I close my book and set it down. I swivel on the bench to face him. "Mouse, back when…I'm sorry I stopped talking to you. I just stopped replying and I never told you why."

"It's okay. You don't owe me an explanation, darling."

"Except that I do. Because I need you to understand," I insist. "I need you to know how much you hurt me."

"Sunshine, I never wanted to hurt you," Mouse says softly. I can tell the subject pains him, and it makes everything I am made of start to ache. "That's why I broke up with you."

"Yeah, well, that hurt. I thought we were going to work. I thought I was just waiting a few months for us to get into the same school, and to graduate and go there together. I was ready to wait for that. And I loved you so much…"

"I loved you too, Sunshine. I loved you enough to let go of you. I didn't want you to feel trapped. Like, what if you met another guy, and you liked him, but felt guilty about it because we were still together, but I wasn't actually there with you. What if you'd found someone who was there, who could love you like you deserved to be loved? What if you just got tired of it? Of me? I had to give you the freedom you deserved."

"You didn't. You didn't have to. I loved you, Mouse. I didn't care about anyone else. All I wanted was for you to love me. As long as I knew that, I could have waited for years. Forever, if I had to. But you gave up on me."

"No, that's not what I did."

"It's exactly what you did, Mouse!" I cry.

"No, Sunshine. No. you aren't listening to me." Mouse sniffs, tips his head back, and sighs. "I loved you, I wanted you to be happy. I didn't want you to feel trapped with a stupid, sad boy living thousands of miles away. And do you have any idea how fucking hard it was knowing that I couldn't just call you, and you'd drop everything to come be with me? How much it killed me that you weren't going to come through my window at two in the morning anymore? I missed you. I missed you so much that it was all I could do. Letting go of you was a way of setting myself free as much as it was setting you free."

"Fuck that, Mouse. If you were really setting yourself free, you would have taken more than a day to send me another email as if nothing had ever happened between us! As if you never loved me."

"Sunshine, did it honestly never occur to you that I kept talking to you because I still loved you? Because I literally couldn't stand to not talk to you."

"You didn't love me enough to give me the time I needed to grieve."

"That *isn't fair*, Sunshine. If you told me you needed time, I would have given it to you."

"Does it not fucking go without saying, Mouse? I mean, you literally went 'Oh, hey Sunshine! I'm breaking up with you, is that cool? It is? Awesome, how was your day?'"

"You know goddamn well shit like that it isn't obvious to me."

"How could it not be? What did you expect?"

"Why didn't you just delete me from your contacts if you didn't want to talk?" Mouse asks angrily.

I've started to cry, and it's so stupid and embarrassing. "Because *I* loved *you* too fucking much to stop talking to you! I could fool myself into thinking we were still together, if we were talking. I didn't...I loved you, Abbot! So much. And you hurt me. And maybe you didn't know, but you did. You did and would you just please accept that? God."

I swipe hot tears from my face and look at Mouse. He blinks at me.

"What?" I ask.

"Nothing. You were just speaking in very angry French."

"Oh, you didn't understand me, did you?"

"I did, actually. I took French all through college. I'm pretty good now."

My lip wobbles. "Bwhat?"

"Yeah. I just remember you always speaking French whenever you were at home, or when you were angry or sad wanted to say something mean to someone without them knowing it, and I just started wondering what you'd been saying, so I took it upon myself to find out."

"*Arrêter d'essayer de me faire comme vous . Je suis très en colère avec vous.*" I groan and drop my face into my hands, crying some more.

Mouse replies in French "Alright, I'm sorry. Sunshine, darling, please don't cry." His voice begs softly, trying to soothe me. But his voice is the kind of voice a boy has when he's trying not to break down. He says in English, "Don't cry. I'm sorry. I was an idiot. I was only eighteen. I'm so sorry I hurt you. I'm so sorry I'm such an insensitive assface. I'm…I didn't deserve you. I'm sorry. Sunshine, you gotta stop crying. Please." Mouse puts his hand on my back and rubs it. I flinch and move away. "Sunshine…"

I wipe my eyes on my sweater sleeves. "I'm gonna. I gotta. I need to go." I jump up from the bench and run to the nearest bathroom.

I lock myself in the handicapped stall and slide to a seat on the floor, pulling my knees into myself and resting my forehead on them. I let myself sob.

This whole thing really shouldn't bother me. It's been over four years since we broke up. I've recovered. I've come to terms with never seeing Mouse again.

But seeing him again, seeing how much like the old Mouse is, and the ways he's matured. Having the chance to tell him exactly what Mouse breaking it off did to me, it's brought up all of this...*This*. And it's so awful. I never wanted to see him again.

I never want to see Mouse Jennings again.

(Mouse)

      I fucked it all up. I feel like a monster for making her cry. For hurting her again. I'd been given this chance to start again with her, and all I did was drive her away again. Sometimes I feel like driving people away is all that I'm good at.

      When she runs off, I slouch against the back of the bench, scrub my face with my hands and push them up into my hair, yanking until I feel the pull.

      This ending is even worse than the first. I can see the damage I've done this time. I saw the tears, and heard her voice break. All of the reasons I didn't break up with her in a phone call or on Skype have come back for me.

      I'm not even sure that I know what happened. It was so fast. I was such an idiot.

      I can't leave it like this again. I have to talk to her. I hate how things ended between us when we were kids. I have to let her know that.

She needs to know how much I regret the mistakes I made about us.

　　I take a minute to collect my thoughts, then I get up from the bench and start to look for her.

　　She needs to know that I regret the end of us.

Chapter Eight

After I collect myself, I splash water on my face and smooth down my hair. I breathe in through my nose until my lungs are all filled with air and breathe it back out shakily. I straighten my sweater and adjust the cross-body strap of my giant bag on my shoulder. I leave the bathroom and pick a random direction to go in.

I walk through the airport making spontaneous turns here and there. I end up in front of the Aviator's Sports Bar. I decide that it's fate, and go inside.

"Miller Lite," I say to the bartender as I slouch over the bar.

"You got ID?" she asks.

"Uh, yeah." I fish in my bag for my wallet, click it open and show her my driver's license.

"Cool," she says, and I close it again. "Bottle or tap?"

"Whatever." I sit down on a barstool and slouch over, folding my arms on the top of the counter.

She slides me a bottle. I twist off the top and take a long drink.

"This whole no-flight thing getting you down?" she asks.

I shrug. "That's kind of the least of my problems," I grumble.

"What other problems have you got?" she asks, leaning over the bar.

"My ex is here."

"Ugh, that blows."

"And I just cried in front of him."

"That blows even harder. Talk to me, girl."

I sigh and tip the Miller bottle onto my lips. "We've been hanging out for the past couple of hours, and it was going fine. We caught up, and all that. But then things started to get deep. I asked him why he didn't drink anymore, and then he told me it was because of his father."

"Oh dear Lord."

"And then I, for whatever ludicrous reason, thought it would be a good idea to talk to him about how much it hurt when we broke up. Because it had started out with us just going out in high school, but then senior year he had to move, so it was long distance. And without any warning, he just called it off. And that wasn't even the worst part. He wanted to jump right into a friendship. Like, he broke up with me, and then he asked me how school was going. God."

"Did the guy defend himself?" asks the bartender. Her name is Laura, according to her crooked name badge,

"He…he said he broke up with me because he didn't want me to feel trapped. He said he was setting me free. But I never felt caged up, you know? The whole thing was so effing unprecedented." I twirl the bottle by its neck, and the base rolls along the counter.

"Mmm-hmm," Laura nods, and picks up a glass and starts wiping it down with a green dishtowel.

I sit quietly for a few minutes, kicking my feet back and forth.

"We promised each other that we were going to wait," I say. "He didn't even try to talk to me about it before he did it. He never *thinks*. Like, it literally did not occur to him that I would need some time to recover after we broke up. He just kept talking to me. And I kept talking back, because I missed him. Because he was so far I could just fool myself into thinking things hadn't changed."

"So I take it you're not over him yet?" she says after she pours a guy a few chairs down a bourbon.

"What? No. I mean yes. I am. I've been over him for years. We're just keeping each other company, that's all."

"So where is he?"

"What?"

"Where's your ex? Are you still hanging out?"

"Oh. No. I…After I started crying, I ran to the bathroom and left him sitting on a bench. I've got no idea where he is now, and I have no desire to find out."

Laura raises her eyebrows. "Are you sure about that?"

"Yes," I say a little too slowly to be sure of myself.

"Really? You are, without a doubt, over this guy?"

"Yes. Yes, I am. It's been five years. I hardly know who he is now." In reality, Mouse has only gotten better.

"What did he do when you started to cry in front of him?"

"He…" His voice. His damn voice. "Listen, I can't be in love with him, okay? He lives in Portland, I live in Chicago, there's not a snowball's chance in hell that I'm ever doing long distance again, and we both want different things out of our lives. M…he doesn't even know what he wants to do yet. And I'm interning, and I'm this close to my story plot getting accepted for the novel writing contest at the publishing house I work at. I'm not gonna throw that away for some boy that broke my heart five years ago, who lives thousands of miles away and more than likely doesn't care about me anymore."

"You're right. That sounds really hard."

"Yeah. I think I just wanna sit here and drink now. Thanks for letting me vent, or whatever."

"Hey, it might as well be part of the job description." Laura half-smiles at me, and then she leaves me alone.

I drop my head into my folded arms and groan.

Two weeks after coffee, we were dating, if you want to be all Facebook official about it. I myself had been calling him my boyfriend in my head after he had called me after dinner the day we'd gone to Starbucks. For the most part, that consisted of the two of us holding hands twenty-four/seven, phone calls that lasted for hours, and him playing with my hair.

It was late November, two and half months since we started going out, and we hadn't even kissed once yet. He just never tried, and I didn't know why.

"Why don't you just kiss him?" My friends in History asked. "You're a feminist, aren't you?"

"That's actually irrelevant," I would say. "He'll kiss me soon. I know he will. He has to."

I didn't know how much longer I could go without kissing him. Every time he smiled at me, it was all I wanted to do. And he smiled at me a lot. Way more than he'd smile at anybody else. (Ha.)

It was a Thursday night. We were supposed to be studying for the Chem quiz tomorrow, but Mouse was learning a song on his guitar and I was watching his beautiful hands mold around the guitar's neck and play with the strings.

"Okay, I think I've got it." He was trying to play the chords to "Moon River". "How's this sound?"

He started to play the song. *Plunk, plunk, plunk, strum. Plunk, plunk, plunk, strum.* Over and over.

"That sounds right," I said. "But now you have to sing it, too."

"You sing. I don't know the chords well enough to sing and play at the same time."

I turned red. "We're supposed to be reviewing chapter eleven."

"Aw, chapter eleven can shove it. For like, thirty more minutes. Just sing with me."

I shook my head.

"Please?"

"Nuh-uh."

"Please, Sunshine."

"No," I laughed.

"What do I have to do to make you sing for me?" Mouse leaned over his guitar and played with my hands. He picked them up and kissed them, raising his eyebrows and looking at me like a puppy begging for scraps.

I tugged my hands from his. "Stop it."

"Tell me. Tell me, tell me. And I'll do it. I promise."

"Smile." I demanded.

He grinned stupidly, his mouth closed and dimples pressing into his cheeks, tucking his chin back into his neck. He waggled his eyebrows at me.

"No, not like that." I snorted, and kicked him softly on the leg.

"Then how?"

"Smile that smile that makes me feel like I've won. The one that shatters glass and blinds unassuming passersby. That one that breaks open your face and makes me stop worrying for a second about why you always seem so sad. Smile the smile that could take over the universe, Mouse. And I'll sing 'Moon River' for you."

Slowly, Mouse's mouth stretched into an ear-to-ear, his teeth showing and upper lip curling like the Joker, but infinitely cuter. His blue eyes crinkled and shined for me, and his cheeks turned a bright and happy pink. He looked so happy he could cry.

"That's the one," I whispered. I smiled too, because it's what I had to do to keep myself from launching at him, crushing Kelly Sue and crashing my lips against his.

"Okay," he breathed, before he placed his fingers where they belonged along the frets and started plunking.

I sang slowly to keep up with his playing, which he did carefully, so he wouldn't mess up. I didn't know the words by heart, so I had to look at the open tab of chords and lyrics, which sucked, because I could only watch him play from my peripheral vision.

"That was beautiful," he said when it was over. "Thank you for singing for me."

I took Kelly Sue out of his hands and put myself there instead, pulling his arms around my waist and laying my head back against his shoulder.

"You're really beautiful, Sunshine. I don't know why you like me."

"Because you're beautiful, too. And…other reasons." I replied.

"Hm." Mouse wrapped his finger around one of my curls. "Your hair is like wool."

"Really."

"Yeah. Like…It's more dense than thick. Like…yarn."

"Are you telling me you want to make a sweater out of my hair?"

"What?! No. No, that isn't what I mean. I just mean it's…"

"Because that's not gonna happen, Hannibal Lecter."

"Hannibal Lecter doesn't make sweaters out of hair. He just eats people."

"You think he'd just waste the body like that? Of course he'd use the hair for a sweater."

"You know what? Forget I said anything. I hate your hair. It sucks."

"Aww, no!" I shoved his shoulder and

giggled.

"I love your hair. I love it." Mouse buried his face in the dark curls. "I love it."

I tossed it all over my shoulder, and it whapped him in the face. He sputtered and pulled strands from his mouth.

"Doesn't taste too great, though."

I twist around in his arms to look at him.

"Mouse?" I ask him.

"Yes?" He pulls away the hair stuck in my eyelashes.

"Why won't you kiss me?"

He drops his hand to my waist. "I didn't think you wanted me to."

"You're my *boyfriend*," I say. "Of course I want you to."

"You want to kiss me?"

"Yes, Mouse. God. I want to kiss you

every time you look at me."

Mouse smiled bashfully and looked down at his lap.

"I want to kiss you, too," he said quietly. "All the time and all over. Anywhere you'll let me."

"Mouse," I took his hands.

"Yeah?"

"Look at me."

Mouse hesitated, and lifted his head for a moment. His lips quivered with embarrassment, and he hung his head again. I tilt his chin up and look at his cloudy blue eyes.

I closed my eyes and pressed my lips to his forehead, right between his eyebrows. I could feel them crease under my mouth. I moved my lips to kiss his eyelids, and then his temples. Mouse sighed and fell forward, his hands pushing into the small of my back. I wound my arms him, my hands splayed on his sides. I kissed his cheeks and his chin.

He laughed and pulled back.

"Sorry," I said, tucking hair behind my ears. "Was that weird?"

"No. It felt really nice. I just want it to be my turn now."

"Oh." I grinned. "Okay."

Mouse wove his fingers into the hair at the either side of my head. He looked at me for a long moment.

"So beautiful," he murmured.

"Mouse."

"Sunshine." He kissed my nose. "My Sunshine."

And then he was kissing my cheeks, and my forehead and behind my ears, which tickled and made my shoulders rise up, so then he kissed those too.

"Sunshine?" Mouse said with a broken voice as he repeatedly kissed me just below the eye.

"Mmm…?" I tried saying his name, but that was all I could manage.

"I think…." He sighed and rested his forehead against mine. "I think I'm going to fall in love with you."

I reached my hands up into his hair, smoothed the tousled curls down and felt my entire body shake with every throb of my heart. I felt my heart everywhere inside of myself: in my hands, in my throat and my stomach, and my head.

"Sunshine?"

"What?"

"Say something?"

"I…" I said, and swallowed. I couldn't talk about loving Mouse. I couldn't talk to him about how he made me feel. I was afraid I would say too much. I cleared my throat. "Can you walk me home?"

"Oh. Uh…yeah, sure." Mouse let go of me and sat back. I scootched away, rubbing a hand over my face.

I put my notes and textbook in my backpack, and Mouse helped me stand up. I didn't let go of his hand, and instead held it tighter, smiling for a short second to cast away the anxious look on his face.

We walked up the basement stairs, I said goodbye to his parents, and after putting on our coats, we went out the front door and out into the cold November.

Mouse pulled our cold hands into the pocket of his wool coat. We walked the five blocks between his house and mine silently. His thumb pressed circles into my palm.

We climbed up the front steps of my split-level house. I stood with my back to the door, and Mouse stood in front of me. The porch light turned his hair a shade that was more red than brown, and made his blue eyes brighter. Like the lights in his head been turned on.

"Well," he said finally, his puff of breath reaching up into the sky. "Um, thanks for coming over."

"Thanks for helping me study," I replied.

The grip Mouse had on my hand relaxed. I took my hand from his pocket, and he folded his arms and looked down at his red high tops. "I didn't help you study. I distracted you with Andy Williams songs," he said guiltily.

"Yeah, I guess you did. But that was a lot more fun than studying."

Mouse chuckled at the ground. He slid his hands into his jeans pockets, and then he looked up at me again. "Have a good night, Sunshine."

Mouse headed back down the steps.

"Hey, Mouse," I called after him.

Mouse turned back around in a slow circle. "Yes?" he said almost inaudibly.

"I think…I'm falling in love with you."

And then I watched something inside of him fall apart. I watched him with level eyes, trying to gauge what he was going to do next.

"Oh, fuck it," he muttered, and bounded back up the steps to me. He snatched me up into his arms, pulling me against his chest. I raised my eyebrows at him.

Mouse blinked once, and then all I was aware of was how cold his face was. How cold all of his face was, except his lips. They were so warm. And so demanding. His mouth pushed against mine, like he was trying to take something out of me. And I kissed back, hoping I was doing it right. I guess I was pretty okay at it, because he didn't stop.

"Mouse," I managed to say. Well. I say managed, but it's more like his name just came out. Like, instead of needing to breathe, I needed to say his name.

And I felt him smile the smile that could take over the universe. And I kissed every crease and corner of his mouth. I wanted to eat that smile. His smile was brighter than the sun; I bet one flash had a whole year's dose of vitamin D in it. It's funny, I remember thinking. That my name was Sunshine and yet it was Mouse that was so bright.

I felt my lungs burn, and I broke away and took a long breath. I guess I must have forgotten to do that.

I looked at my boyfriend. His eyes were still closed, and he was sort of slouched over, like he was asleep standing up. I was certain that I could knock him over with a single poke in the arm.

"Mouse?"

His eyes snapped open. "What?"

"It's time for you to go home."

"Oh." He stood up straighter. "Yeah. You're right. I should go."

"Don't walk into any oncoming traffic, please."

Mouse smiled like a lovestruck cartoon character. "I won't."

I kissed the stupid smile off his face. "Now go home, you crazy boy."

"Yes, ma'am." He turned and walked down the stairs with quick, loose-limbed steps.

"Sleep tight, my huckleberry friend," I said just loud enough for him to hear at the end of my driveway.

"G'night," Mouse called over his shoulder, looking at me and not at the curb, which he tripped over. I stifled a snort and watched him walk away before I went inside.

I finished my homework and spent the rest of the night drawing pictures of Mouse in the sketchbook my father gave me for my birthday while listening to the Audrey Hepburn version of "Moon River" on repeat.

    I fell asleep with the words of the song still in my ears.

Chapter Nine

I'm sitting with my empty Miller bottle now, staring at the stains and scratches on the bar. The noise of a football game on one TV and the news on another mingles together with cacophonous chaos. And it smells, well, like a bar. I hate it. And I completely understand Mouse's aversion to such places.

Mouse.

I should really get out of here. But where would I go? To another godforsaken store selling stupid Colorado souvenirs? To Jamba Juice? Soon the shops are all going to close and all I'll have to keep me busy will be my laptop and my books. Watching everything lock up would be like being stuck in a mall after hours.

I pay for my beer, and hop off the bar stool and get out of the place. I shove my cold hands in the pockets of my peacoat and walk up to one of the departure boards. There's been no change.

I find a fairly desolate row of uncomfortable plastic chairs, and decide to set up camp there. I put my bag in one seat, and stretch out on my stomach on three other ones. I get my book from my bag and start to read it, but the words start to mean nothing to me, so I put it away and reach for my MacBook instead.

After I get WiFi access, I check my Twitter feed and my email, and scroll through Pinterest for an hour. I stare at a black and white photography of a girl and her boyfriend for way too long. I close Pinterest and browse through Netflix instead.

Nothing, not even the things in my queue appeal to me, but I keep clicking around anyway, reading the movie and TV show summaries.

I get bored with this after a while and fold down the screen of my laptop. I sit up and stretch. When I open my eyes, they fall on the person I was trying very hard to avoid.

And wouldn't you know it: He looks

right at me.

I jump up immediately, shoving my laptop in my bag and hefting it onto my shoulder. And now I'm stuck between fight and flight.

Before I get to choose, Mouse is walking towards me. I fold my arms and wait for him. He stands in front of me, his hands deep in the pockets of his cardigan, stretching it out. He stares at me. I stare back, but don't say anything to him.

"What if I told you I regret it?" he says.

"Regret what?" I reply monotonously.

"The stupid shit I did when I was eighteen. Breaking up with you. What if I told you I regretted it?"

"What difference does that make now, Mouse? You still did it. You can't go back and change it."

"No, but like, I wish I never broke up with you."

"Mouse, no. Stop."

His voice plows right over mine. "I regret listening to my dad, who said it wouldn't last, that you'd meet someone else and sleep with him behind my back—"

"Mouse! Stop it."

"What if I said that I wish I waited, I wish that we had picked a college to go to together, and I wish I got to keep a countdown to the day when I got to see you again and we'd run to each other across the quad, or whatever."

"Please stop."

"What if I said that I—"

"Mouse, no. You need to stop talking."

"You're not listening."

"Of course I'm not. I can't listen to this. Your regrets change nothing. Stop. Leave."

"I'm not gonna leave again."

"Mouse, oh my God. There is no 'again'. I have a life now. I'm not…No. There's nothing. Just stop."

Mouse opens his mouth again.

"STOP." I interrupt him. "I'm not interested in talking with you about our past anymore. If you want to hang out, we're going to have to stop talking about this."

"I don't want to stop," he says.

"Then leave me alone. Because I'm not going to let you do this to me. I'm not going to do this to *myself*."

"Do what, Sunshine?" Mouse asks, his voice sad and weary.

"I'm not going to fool myself again. Into thinking that I can make this work. We can't work. I don't…I'm through with romance. I don't need this right now."

Mouse breaks eye contact, finally. He looks away, and a shadow passes over his face.

"You know what I regret, Mouse?"

He says nothing.

"I regret ever seeing you again."

He bites his lip, hard, and he seems smaller.

I hate the words I just said. And I hate the words I say next. "Have a nice life, Mouse. I hope you get your shit together before your life passes you by. You've done it once. Go9d knows what'll happen to you if you do it again."

And then I leave. And I don't think, not even for a second, about looking back.

Chapter Ten

I was on my way to meet Mouse so we could both walk to my house when I heard his ringtone ("Transcendental Youth" by The Mountain Goats) go off from where my phone was tucked safely in my pocket. I took it out and answered it.

"Hello?"

"Hey, Sunshine."

"Hey. I'm on my way. Sorry, I had to stop and talk to my AP Lit teacher." I say as I walk down the emptying halls. "I'll meet you outside, okay?"

"Actually, about that. I have a proposition for you."

"Okay…"

"How about instead of going over to your house right now, we audition for the talent show?"

"Coffee Shop auditions are today. Isn't it too late to sign up?"

"..."

"Mouse?"

"I may or may not have signed us up already."

"Mouse!"

"Sorry! I'm sorry, I should have told you."

"Uh, *yeah*." I entered the commons, and I could see Mouse leaning against a wall, playing with a sticker on Kelly Sue's case and looking out a window.

"But what do you think?"

"I think you should have told me before...when is our hypothetical audition?"

"3:05."

"Mouse...! It's..." I checked the clock

on the wall. "It's almost three now!"

"I know. I'm the worst."

I sighed and hung up as I approached him. He saw me and turned around.

"What would we even sing?"

"Well, I polished up 'Moon River'…"

"But I don't know all the words to that song."

"I printed them off."

"That song is so short, though. Nobody will remember us."

"That isn't the point, Sunshine.'"

"Oh, it isn't? Was the point to keep this whole idea of auditioning for the talent show from me?"

"No, Sunshine. I'm sorry I didn't tell you. Okay, look. If it makes you feel better, I'll let you pick the song instead."

I thought for a minute. "Do you know 'Landslide'?"

Mouse smiled. "Yeah. I love that song."

"Of course you do."

"Do you wanna sing that?"

"Yeah. I mean…it's. Yes."

"Okay. We've got fifteen minutes before our audition. Let's practice."

We sat in the plastic chairs standing around one of the cafeteria tables. Mouse took out Kelly Sue and took a second to make sure she was tuned.

Fifteen minutes later we stood in front of the door to the black box, where auditions were taking place. I must have looked nervous (which I was), because Mouse reached over and took my hand.

"You're gonna do great. I know you are."

"What if we don't get in?" I said.

"Then you don't have to perform in front of a hundred people. You don't really have anything to lose here."

I grumbled.

"Hey." Mouse squeezed my hand.

I looked at him. "What?"

"Thank you for doing this, Sunshine. It really does mean a lot to me."

"Even if we don't get in?"

"Even then. I just really like that I can share this part of me with you like this."

I felt my mouth stretch into a weak smile. We were still looking at each other when the door to the black box opened and we were told to come in.

A couple of days later, we saw the set

list on the wall outside the black box. Our names were sitting at the bottom of the list. Mouse was so happy that he kissed me hard in front of God and everyone, even though public displays of affection were against the rules.

    After we got told off by the hall monitor, Mouse kissed me again as soon as she turned her back. It was probably just out of spite, but not one single cell of me minded.

Chapter Eleven

I don't go very far because I am really tired of walking. I round the corner, and sit against the wall. It takes him approximately forty seconds to find me.

"Mouse, what did I just get done telling you?" I bark when I see his old red Converse walk up to me.

"You said I can't talk about us breaking up anymore if I want to hang out with you."

"So what are you still talking to me for?"

"Because I'm not gonna talk about our breakup anymore. I'm sorry for what went down back there. I'll be good. You can punch me if I'm not."

"Hmm. Tempting."

"Come on." His hand appears in front of my face. "Get up. I'll buy you dinner. In the least date-ish way I know how to."

I sigh melodramatically and take his hand. Mouse pulls me to my feet. The first thing my eyes settle on is his face. He looks tired. His eyes aren't as clear as they were before, and there's bags underneath them. He's smiling, but it's all wrong. He lets go of my hand immediately, and we walk to the least romantic eating facility we can find—McDonald's.

There isn't much to talk about now that we're pretending we were never in a relationship. We talk about the weather, and our families, and our favorite places in the cities we live in. My favorite place is Navy Pier, and Mouse's favorite place is Powell's City of Books, where he works.

After we finish eating, we watch Mouse's favorite movie (*Charlie Bartlett*) on my laptop on a couch at the south end of the airport.

"This Charlie guy looks freakishly like you," I say at the beginning of the movie.

"People say that all the time. I mean, I

guess he's a pretty good looking guy."

As we get further into the film, I come to the realization that not only does Mouse look like Charlie Bartlett (Anton Yelchin, Mouse says the actor's name is) but he is eerily similar in personality as well. I mean, Mouse was never a dealer of prescription drugs. But they do have the same sense of humor. Frankly, it's a little terrifying.

"Did you change your name when you moved, and become an actor? Or, was the whole moving thing just a cover so I wouldn't find about your top secret acting career? Is 'Anton Yelchin' your stage name or something?" I ask.

"Damn it, I was hoping you would never find me out." Mouse goes along with me.

When the movie is over, I open up a browser window and log on to YouTube. I read the comments on my latest upload. There's over a hundred, so I only reply to a few of them.

"Are our cover videos still up there?"

"Not here, this is my BookTube channel. The cover videos are private on my vlogging channel." I explain.

"Oh. Hey, can we watch one?"

"What? No." I never watch my videos after I edit them. I hate listening to my voice.

"But I wanna see what your life is like."

"Then watch them by yourself."

"But then I can't make fun of you," Mouse complains.

"Oh, well in that case..." I say sarcastically.

"If I can't watch you watch your past-self talk about books and whatever else and laugh at your embarrassment, watching your videos would not be nearly as fun."

"Excuse you. My videos are plenty of fun."

"Sure, if your idea of fun is talking at a camera for an hour about books."

"Yes." I snap my computer shut. "It is."

There's a long pause.

"I don't...I was kidding. I'm sure your videos are awesome, Sunshine," Mouse says.

I look at him for a long time. I know he was kidding, but he looks so sorry about it. Like he'll never forgive himself if I don't forgive him myself.

"It's...it's okay, Mouse. I know you wouldn't...I know. It's okay."

His face rests. "Do you wanna go for a walk?"

I start to nod, but my mind suddenly is overcome with the task of yawning.

"Oh, 'm sorry," I say sleepily. "I guess jetlag is finally catching up with me."

"Yeah?"

"Yeah. I think…I'm gonna take a nap. You can take a walk if you want. I mean. Obviously. But I'm gonna stay here. And sleep."

Mouse starts to reply, but I'm already dozing off, so I can hardly hear what he says.

Chapter Twelve

Mouse used to talk a lot about all the reasons he wasn't worth loving. He'd always said he wasn't a good person, that he was too fucked up, all these terrible things. I guess Mouse knows himself better than I do, or at least in the sense that he knew what went on in that mind of his, and I only knew what went on in there when he would tell me. But all the things he told me never made him seem like a bad person. I mean, he wasn't perfect either, he was far too oblivious to be perfect. But he was never bad. Insensitive, sure. But not on purpose. Never on purpose. He was just a little different than most people that way. I used to think it was some form of autism, but I never really wanted to ask.

To tell the truth, I was a little afraid of that side of him. Learning what really went on his head. I was afraid that it was a mess, that he would scare me. I was scared of him wanting to hurt himself. I was afraid of the life he had when I wasn't with him. I wasn't afraid of the mess, but I was afraid of him being so absorbed in the mess that he would start thinking he didn't have the capacity to love, or to be good anymore.

But the thing about Mouse, the one thing I know about him that he doesn't, is that he is so very good. He's a good friend, a good listener, good at keeping quiet, good at speaking up, good at being Mouse. Good at being someone worthy of being called Mouse. Good at being quiet, small and harmless. Good at scaring people just by being around. That last one doesn't sound like very good trait to have, but Mouse is that and all of them and I am so glad for it.

Or was.

I *was* glad for it. Now it doesn't matter to me anymore.

Not a bit. Not at all.

Not at all do I care about good, good Mouse and his blue ribbon smile.

Chapter Thirteen

When I wake up from my nap, I find Mouse stretched out next to me, my laptop resting on his stomach, and a pair of headphones over his ears.

I sit up immediately. "Why are you on my laptop?"

"You really should put a password on this thing. Anyone could just open the lid and look you up on YouTube while you're asleep." Mouse looked over at me and smirked.

"MOUSE!" I try to snatch the laptop back from him, but his grip is firm.

"Careful, Sunshine. Do you know how much one of these cost?"

"Of course I know, I bought that myself."

"On Craigslist."

"From the Apple Store, you ass." I grab

at it again.

"Christ, Sunny, how much is this internship paying you?"

"I saved up for it."

"Uh-huh," Mouse clicks play on another video. "You know, I really liked the one...the vlog with the tour of Chicago."

"You watched *Thoughts from Chicago*?"

"Yeah. The cinematography was pretty good."

"...What others did you watch?" I ask warily.

"I watched most of them, actually."

"Most of them? How long was I out?" I check my phone for the time.

"It's almost nine." Mouse says, sliding the headphones off.

"And you've just been lying next to me

with my laptop, watching all of the videos I have ever put on YouTube?"

"Well, I got up once to go to the bathroom. But I brought your laptop with so no one would steal it while you were sleeping," Mouse says.

"Hm," I say stiffly. And then, with a sharp intake of breath, I fully realize the way we're positioned on this couch. I'm laying down, my legs stretched out to the other side. And Mouse is lying down too, so I am sandwiched between him and the back of the couch. His head is propped up on the arm of the couch. His bow legs are jumbled together with my shorter, thicker legs. We're lying down together.

The last time the two of us were in a predicament anything like this one was the night, or early, early morning before Mouse moved away. I had walked to his house in the middle of the night because I couldn't sleep. Mouse was leaving in the morning and it was all I could think about.

I'd come into his basement bedroom through the window. I remember that my shirt had ridden up, and before he helped me reach the floor, he pulled my shirt down gently. Like, he could have just pulled me down like that, with my bare stomach showing; he could have touched me there; I wouldn't even have cared. But he did care, he must have. He cared enough to pull my shirt back down before he touched me.

And then, when we were both standing on the nubby carpet floor, our fingers pressing into each other's sides and back, he kissed me once, and I said "I love you", and he said "I love you" back.

And then he let go of me and walked over to his bed, falling down clumsily onto it, and scrubbing his hands all over his face.

"I don't want tomorrow to come," he mumbled.

"It's two in the morning," I said back ruefully. "It is tomorrow."

"Shit."

"Shit is right," I sat on the edge of his bed.

"So that's…" Mouse counted in his head. "Ten hours before I leave."

Before he'd leave. Me. This place. This good little world we'd built for ourselves.

"Your math is dead on, I'm afraid."

Mouse, who had previously been looking at the ceiling, turned his head to look at me.

"Why is this happening, Sunshine?" he asked me softly.

I lay down next to him. "Because life isn't fair."

"Yeah, okay, but why can't life not be fair in a different way? Like, what if instead of moving, I just had a week's detention, or broke my leg, or got beat up in an after-school fight or something?"

Mouse was known to get himself into a scuffle or two. On the occasions when he was angry. When he gave people a real reason to be afraid of him.

"Mouse, no more fights. We talked about this." Lately, I'd been able to rope him in when he'd gotten riled up.

"I'm speaking hypothetically, here."

"Would you really rather have another black eye or bloody nose than move away?"

"Yes, absolutely. I would willingly get the shit kicked out of me if it meant I got to stay here and be with you," Mouse said emphatically. "I would also break my leg or take a week's worth of detention. Maybe even two weeks."

"Wow, *two* weeks of detention? I'm flattered, Mouse." I grinned at him.

His blue ribbon grin almost crossed his face. He said, "Don't let it go to your head."

I laughed softly and put my head on his

chest. He rubbed my shoulder and looked back up at the ceiling.

"God, I'm gonna miss you," Mouse sighed. "I'm gonna miss you so fucking much."

I could feel myself unravel. "Mouse…"

"Sunshine, I…" He breathed in through his nose, making a sniffly noise.

"Mouse, oh my god, *stop*. I didn't come here so we could be all weepy together. I just came so we could be together." I took his face in my hands and kissed him softly. "I don't want to think about what happens ten hours from now. I don't want to think about anything like that. I don't want to *think*. I just want to make out with you." I kissed him again, longer, then moved back to look at his face. I ran my thumb over his cheek. "Alright?"

For the longest time, Mouse just stared at me. He looked lost and scared. His eyes desperately searched my face, and mine searched his.

Then he reached his large, warm hand

up and put it on the back of my neck. He brought me closer, looking at me one moment longer before closing his eyes and pressing his lips to mine. I move to settle on top of him, pushing my tongue into his mouth. My fingers brushed the hair near his temples. Mouse's arms wound tightly around me, and as he pressed me into him, I could feel something deep inside of him shake, as if the thought of letting go of me gave him a panic attack. I broke away from him and put my mouth next to his ear.

"Hey," I whispered. "It's okay. You're okay. Everything is going to be okay." I kissed behind his ear and down his neck. The shaking inside of him stopped, and I felt his body relax into the mattress. I ran my lips down his throat, and a high, weak noise came from it.

"You're okay," I said again, kissing his closed eyes, and his mouth again.

Mouse pushed himself up like a baby deer trying to get used to its legs, and leaned against the headboard of his bed. He pulled me onto his lap, and put his hands on my sides, underneath my shirt. His lips moved across mine, soft and sleepy.

"Sunshine?" he rasped with his face buried in my neck.

"Mmm?" My shoulders rose with drowsy pleasure.

He lifted his face so I could look at him. His hair was tousled and his face was red, and his neck was splotchy.

"I don't think…I don't think I want to stop. I want to be with you like this. I want you like this. Like now or never." His eyes were wild, and they didn't rest on one part of my face for more than half a second.

I held his chin in my hand to steady him. "Never say never, sweet boy." I shut my eyes and touched my forehead to his.

He jutted his chin forward to kiss me. "Okay." He rested his forehead on my sternum. "I want to be with you Sunshine. I want you this way now, and all night long."

I played with his hair at the back of his neck, and nuzzled my face in the hair at the top of his head. "I want that, too. I want you until the sun comes up."

Mouse brought his head back up, and there was the blue ribbon grin. He took my hands and led them to the hem of his shirt. I curled my fingers around it and brought the black and white baseball tee over his head. I tossed it on the floor, and I lifted my arms above my head. Mouse rolled the hem of my shirt up and up, until it was off, and he put it on the floor with his. He kissed me in a way I never thought he would, and we lay back down, with me on top of him. I closed my eyes, and forgot about the cardboard boxes all around his room filled with all of his things, and forgot about everything but getting closer, and closer, closer to him.

That was the last time I lay down with Mouse. Until right now.

It occurs to me that perhaps I should sit

up. I shouldn't be lying down with him, not if it brings up such memories. But I'm too tired to move, so I stay there. Mouse looks at me, and it feels like being felt. As if he is holding my face or rubbing my arm. And his eyes burrow into me, and make a home right in my center. I swallow and look right back. He smiles lazily.

"That face," he says.

"What?" It comes out a whisper.

"That face—the one you're making now—I used to love that face. I fell in love with you the first time you looked at me with that face. I mean, I was already falling—hard, so hard. And then you made that face, and…" Mouse makes an exploding noise. "I was a goner."

I can feel myself blush, so I look away. Down at his guitar, and then around at the mostly empty section of the airport we are in.

"Hey, that grumpy security guard is gone. And there's nobody to watch us. Do you wanna play some more music?"

Mouse sits up and looks around. "Sure. Velvet Underground, 'After Hours'? I play, you sing?"

"After Hours" was one of the many songs that we had memorized. I'm pretty sure I remember it.

"Okay. One, two, three…"

It's weird, how easy it is to fall into our old selves when we make music together. I smile more when we're singing that I feel I've smiled in weeks.

Just as the song ends, my phone rings.

"Huh. Weird. It's my boss. I should take this. Sorry." I answer the call and jump up from the bench and take a few steps away from Mouse.

"Soleil, it's Jolene."

"I know. What's going on?"

"Where are you right now?"

"I'm at Denver International Airport.

None of the flights are leaving; there's a crazy snowstorm. Why, do you need me?"

"Well, no, you're vacation is two days longer. I just wanted to tell you that I was looking over your submission for the publishing contest."

"Oh?" The interns at Pad & Pen are always given the option to enter a story for an annual publishing contest. After the plot is accepted, the long process of creating the story begins, which is usually where people start dropping out. The company will pick from the completed stories one book to have edited and published. There's over fifty interns at the Chicago headquarters. I submitted a story my first year working at Pad & Pen, which in retrospect was a horrible story to submit, and didn't even make it into the first round. I submitted a new story idea (the one I'd been plotting for a while) a few weeks before Christmas vacation and I'm feeling a lot better about this one.

"Yes," Jolene says. "Your plot is intriguing, and I'm offering you the opportunity to participate in the publishing competition."

I've heard wrong; I'm sure of it. "What?"

"Your book plot has been accepted into the competition. Would you like to participate?"

"Er—I mean, yes! Yes, of course I do. Oh my goodness, really?"

"Yes, it's such a fresh perspective, and I'm interested in seeing where you go with it. It's a really alternative outlook on the idea of love, and I am excited to see where your character ends up at the end of the book."

Frankly, so was I. "I…thank you. Thank you so much."

"Wonderful. See you next week, Soleil." I'm Soleil now, everywhere but with my family and Mouse.

"Yes. See you. Thank you. Goodbye."

"Bye, hope the plane thing gets sorted soon." Jolene hangs up.

I stare down at my phone and marvel at the amazing possibilities this year now contains.

After a minute, I put my phone back in my pocket and sit back down with Mouse. He's plucking away at a song I don't recognize.

"Everything okay?" he asks.

"Hm? Oh, yeah. Yeah everything is…great."

"Good." He start strumming, and I sit sideways on the couch, crossing my legs and watching him.

Chapter Fourteen

Mouse and his guitar playing is a good 67% of the reason I fell in love with him. One time he stole my iPod and learned all of my most played songs in a week and performed them for me on my birthday.

The look on his face when he sang and played Kelly Sue was dreamy. Music was this special part of him, and he would just get so lost in it. It was like he didn't know or notice the world around him when he played. And then, he'd look right at me, after the song was over, with this expression like he'd just woken up from sleeping. Or like he had been daydreaming, and a teacher had just shouted his name in class. Mouse almost never looked right at me when he sang. Not even on my birthday.

The one time he did was one week after he'd moved. We were having a Skype date, and right before he hung up to go to sleep, because he was three hours ahead of me, he got out his guitar and sang 'Rivers and Roads' to me. He didn't break eye contact once. His voice broke three times. We were both crying by the end.

    The night Mouse told me he was moving, I ignored his calls three times. I'd told him that day after school that I had a big group project, and predictably, I got tasked with most of the work. The project was due in the morning, and I had countless things to do, so I told him not to call me that night. Whenever Mouse called, which was most nights, we always ended up having conversations that lasted for hours. I didn't have the time to linger on the line and quote entire movies with my boyfriend on that particular night.

    So when he called the first time, I just declined it. I thought he just forgot. But then he called again, and again. I almost picked up to tell him not to call, but I didn't want to look up at the clock and see that two hours had gone by, so I just hung up on him. The third time, he left a voicemail, which he never does, because he hates them, and I always pick up, so he never has to.

"Sunshine…," the voicemail said. "Sunshine. Something's wrong. Everything is so wrong. I can't…they didn't even ask. And we're…Sunshine, I don't know what to do. It's bad, Sunshine. It's so bad. I need help. I know you're really super busy, but I need to talk to you. I wouldn't be asking if wasn't an emergency. Sunshine…," He was crying by now. "I'm so scared. Call me back. I need to talk to you."

When Mouse cried, I knew it had to be bad. So I dropped my glue stick and called him back.

"Mouse?" I said as soon as the ringing stopped.

"Sunshine."

"Hi, sorry I kept declining. I was just—"

"You were working. I know. I'm sorry."

"No, it's okay. What's going on?"

"I'm…we're moving."

"What?"

"To Wisconsin. In the middle of the summer. We're moving. Because Dad's job is transferring. All of us, we're just going. I'm leaving, Sunshine."

"The middle of the summer?" It was only a few weeks until summer started. That gave us only two or three months.

"Yeah. God, I'm…I am so angry at him. I mean…I've got one more year of high school. And he isn't even getting a raise or anything. It's just a new position. He didn't have to take it, but he did. And now I'm not gonna see you again."

"Hey, now. Don't talk like that. That's not true. We can still go to college together. It's only a year." My mind was going a mile a minute; everything was falling apart so fast, and all I could think of was making quick fixes. Saying what I wanted to be true.

"It's not 'only', Sunshine. It's a whole fucking year. I'm not coming back for Christmas or spring break or anything. I am going to live in Wisconsin." I knew his face was red, and his neck was splotchy and that there were hot tears running down his face.

The way he spoke scared me. "Mouse…do you want to…break up?"

"What? No! No, I don't want to do that. I'm not breaking up with you. No. I can't."

"Okay. So we're gonna make it work. Right, Mouse? …Mouse."

He wasn't replying.

"Mouse?"

"I'm not going."

"What—Mouse?"

"I'll stay here. I'll think of something. I'm not going. I can't go."

I could hear irregular breathing through the receiver.

"Mouse, you need to calm down."

"Mouse, come over. Come to my house.

I'll make tea. Just come over here. Don't do anything crazy."

Fifteen minutes there was a knock at the door. I ran to answer it before my parents would wake up. It was already almost eleven.

Mouse eyes were bloodshot and had circles around them. His hair was frizzy and frazzled, and I knew he'd been yanking his fingers through it. His face seemed empty.

"Hey, sorry. My parents are sleeping so we're gonna have to be super quiet." I moved back to let him in. "Just go in my room. I'm gonna make tea and find a snack and I'll be down there soon, okay?"

Mouse walked slowly down the hall to my room. I came in five minutes later to find him sprawled out on my bed, lying face down. I set the mugs on my desk next to the bed.

"Mouse?"

He rolled over and looked at me with bleary eyes.

"I'm sorry," I knelt beside him. I almost moved my hand to touch him, but he didn't particularly look like he wanted to be touched. "Do you want to talk?"

"No," he said hoarsely.

"Okay. Well…I'm gonna be on the floor over here, working. And if you need to talk, we can talk. Okay?"

He didn't respond. I frowned, picked up my mug and an Oreo and went back to work.

Mouse was quiet for half an hour. This was the part of Mouse that scared me. I had a vague idea of why he was upset, but whatever went on inside of his head I was completely unaware of. I didn't know how bad it was. It was with a lingering pang in my stomach that I decorated my tri-fold board.

My tea was gone and I was writing a five page lab report when Mouse finally made a noise. It started as a long squeak and then turned into low, hard sobs.

"Mouse?" I looked up from my computer at him. He was on his side, with his back to me, and his body shook with each heavy sob. I scrambled to my feet and went around the bed to him. His eyes were squeezed shut. "Hey, hey. Mouse…it's okay." I crawled onto the bed and sat on my feet. Mouse rolled onto his stomach.

I didn't really know what to do, so I just stretched out on to the bed, on my side, and rubbed his back while he cried. And that's all I did for an hour, until I knew he was sleeping, and his body got still and his breath was slower.

I got up carefully and crawled to the end of the bed to take off his shoes. I put them on the floor and went back to work on my project. I was exhausted and worried about Mouse, so for minutes at a time I would just sit and stare at all the work that surrounded me. I didn't finish everything until six in the morning. I woke up Mouse, and we walked to school together after making a ten minute stop at his house to get his books and so he could change his clothes. His parents never noticed he was gone.

I fell asleep in class, and when it was my group's turn to present, it was a stumbling mess. By some miracle, we got a B minus. All I could think about for the entire day was sleep and Mouse.

When I met him after school, he looked even worse than he had last night. His face was ashy and a scowl seemed to be permanently stuck on his face. We didn't talk at all on the bus ride to his house.

When we got there, we listened to music and lay on his bedroom floor. I would have fallen asleep, were it not for the fact that we were listening to metal (his pick, not mine) and I couldn't stop worrying about him.

After half an hour of incoherent screaming, I go up and turned the music off. Mouse tilted his head back from his spot on the floor to look at me.

"Why did you do that?" he asked

slowly.

"Because metal music is the worst. But mostly because you aren't talking to me, and you should be." I sat down against his dresser.

Mouse stared at the ceiling some more. "About what?"

"About why moving to Wisconsin is so upsetting to you."

"Why shouldn't it upset me?" asked Mouse.

"I'm not saying it shouldn't. I would be upset if I found out I was moving away, too. I just want to know why it is upsetting to you, personally."

Mouse sighed. I waited for him to say something.

"We've moved so many times. And he promised this would be the last time. So I let myself slow down, settle in. I let myself get comfortable. Which is always a mistake with him.

But I was so sure. I was so sure that I let myself ask you out. And you made me feel so safe and good, Sunshine. I'm happy being with you.

"And now there's this, and it makes me angry. Like, he couldn't have waited one year for me to finish high school before he decided to take on a new job? He knew how good this place was for me, for all of us, really. And he's just pulled the rug out from under our feet. And I mean, it's not just me that's mad about this. Mom is, too. They were fighting when I called you last night. And we all know Dad is going to win. Laney doesn't have much to lose, but Gloria was just starting to make good friends. I'm so angry at him for doing this to us."

Mouse sat up, hunching his shoulders and picking at the carpet. "There. That's why."

"I don't know what to say to any of that."

"Don't say anything, then. Actually, I…I'm really not interested in talking about it anymore. I'm just going to ignore it for as long as

I can."

"Mouse, are you sure that's a good idea?"

"No," he said, his voice equal parts gentle and taut. "But it's all I can manage right now."

There was a long, excruciating silence. I felt like I wouldn't be able to breathe until I said something else.

"Hey, Mouse?"

"Yeah?"

"I love you."

He lifted his head and half of his mouth smiled. "Thanks. You, too."

"Do you wanna go to the park?"

"Yeah. Being in this house is making me crazy."

Chapter Fifteen

It's almost ten now. We got up a while ago to stretch our legs. We're standing in front of a floor to ceiling window, staring out at the snow that's still falling down.

"It's beautiful," I say. "In Chicago it all turns to slush before you really get to admire it."

"Yeah, Portland's kind of allergic to snow. We never get much, and when we do, it melts or gets all dirty pretty fast."

"Hmm. I wish we could go out in it."

"And do what?"

"I don't know. Catch snowflakes on our tongues. Dance, run around."

Mouse blinks at me then breaks into a run. He jumps and spins in wide, drunken circles with his arms spread wide, and I'm struck by his wingspan.

"What are you doing?" I ask as he

passes me.

He skips backwards to reply to me. "What does it look like I'm doing?"

"Um, having a psychotic episode?"

"I'm dancing in the snow!"

"Mouse, oh my god, stop. People can see you." The few people in the south end are dozing off, and only some of them are watching him.

"So? Get out here, Sunshine! This was your idea."

"Not quite." I raise my eyebrows as he tips his head back to catch imaginary snowflakes on his tongue.

Mouse runs to me and takes my hands.

"Come on," he says through ragged breaths. "Dance in the snow with me."

I sigh and let him pull me towards the huge windows where we can see the snow fall.

We spin in circles like Jack and Kate in *Titanic*, and then we start dancing, slow dancing.

"I just remembered something," Mouse says.

"What's that?"

"We never got to go to prom together."

Prom was in May, a few months after we'd broken up. "You're right," I say as Mouse twirls me. "We didn't."

"Did you go with somebody else?"

"I went with my friends. It was okay. All the music sucked."

"That's to be expected."

"Did you go?"

"Oh, no. I stayed home and played video games."

"You probably didn't miss much."

Half a smile appears on Mouse's face.

We sway quietly for a minute.

"What did you wear?" he asks.

"What?"

"To prom. What did you wear to prom?"

"Oh. It was this floor length white, lacy number. It had a corset and a full skirt. My logic was, that if I wasn't going to have a date to prom, I was going to make all the boys wish that they'd asked me."

"I bet you looked amazing."

"I looked pretty good. My hair was in this crazy elaborate updo. I wasn't allowed to touch my head all night. Not that I could have; I had fake nails on."

"Ah," Mouse's eyes crinkle as he grinned. I watch snowflakes fall outside. Soon the eye contact becomes too much, and I look away.

"We didn't even go to homecoming together," I say.

"That's because homecoming is totally overrated and not a once in a lifetime experience."

"Prom is overrated too. Seriously, all they fed us was butter mints and watered-down Italian sodas."

"Well, I'm glad I didn't go, then."

"Besides, I wouldn't have gone with a date, anyway."

"Why not?"

"We'd just broken up. I wasn't ready to date anybody else yet."

"We broke up right before Christmas vacation."

"I still wasn't over you. It took me a really long time to be over you."

"Oh." Mouse frowns. "Yeah, I guess that makes sense."

We dance quietly for a few moments.

"So what was that phone call you got all about?" Mouse asks me.

"It was my boss at Pad & Pen."

"What did your boss want to tell you? Did you get a raise?"

"I wish," I snorted. No, um…I submitted this story idea for a contest the publishing company has for all the interns every year, and it got accepted."

"So what does that mean?"

"It means I get to expand it into a book and if they decide it's good enough, I get help polishing it and then it gets published."

"So you're getting a chance to have a book you wrote made into a real book other people can read?"

I nod and smile. "Yeah. Isn't it amazing?"

"It's great! It's everything you ever wanted. I'm really proud of you, Sunshine."

"Thank you," I say.

"So, what's it going to be about?"

"The book? Um...it's about a girl who fell in love with a boy who didn't love her well enough, and how it affects her image of herself, and her idea of what love is."

"I see. Is it um...written from experience?" Mouse asks carefully.

For a long time, I try to find a good answer. "I used to think that it was. When submitted it, I thought that it was. I guess my experience wasn't telling the whole story."

"It was telling the story you thought you knew. That's what an experience is. Which isn't bad, I don't think. It leaves room for character development."

"Yeah, you're right. When did you get so smart?"

"Hey, I was an English major for a little bit, remember? I know some stuff."

"Oh good, only some stuff. Just as long as I'm still the one who know most stuff."

"That burden remains on you, yes," Mouse laughs. "So have you started writing it yet?"

"Um, I've got a couple of chapters written. I don't think they're that good yet."

"Can I read them?"

"While I sit quietly wondering what you think of my horrible, unfinished first draft? I don't think so."

"Well, how about you read it to me, then?"

"Hm."

"Please?"

"Well, okay. But you can't judge it too much because it's messy and sort of sad and stuff."

"It's a deal."

"Okay." I drop my hands from his shoulders and got back to the couch. Mouse sits next to me, leaning back, settling in.

"Okay, so this is just the prologue. Um, it's written in first person from a girl's perspective. Uh…obviously. It's mostly inner monologue this early in. I uh. Here we go, I guess."

The phrase 'well-loved' never made much sense to me. Because if someone can be loved well, then one must assume someone can also be loved poorly. And loving poorly can't really be loving at all. Being loved well should just mean that someone is loved.

So, using my logic, I guess I never was loved by him. Because love doesn't just up and leave. Love tries, and I know he didn't. Maybe it wasn't his fault, maybe he just wasn't strong enough. But when it happened, the way it did, I knew I wasn't well-loved by him. I knew that, and I let it eat at me. And it still does, picking away at my heart and my head. It makes me think that I did something wrong, and now that the thought's eaten at me, there's nothing left that anybody else can love, assuming there ever was something there to love at all.

Anyway, that was the mindset I had as I sat on the couch upside-down on the rainiest Saturday of the year. It seemed to be the only mindset I had these days. This concerned my friends, and being the fantastic people they were, they told my parents. This news concerned them as well, so after a long, uncomfortable talk, we had decided that I had to start going to therapy.

And that couch? It was in the therapist's office. Yes, not only did they decide I had to go to therapy, but on Saturday. A Saturday morning, at that.

Since it was the first meeting, we didn't go too deep. I couldn't have formed a complete thought anyway, I was so tired. And so bored. So many things.

And all of the things I was now—crazy,

depressed, exhausted, broken—I was because of him. Because him and how poorly he loved me.

I look up from my laptop and sigh. Mouse is staring ahead blankly. He's slouched low on the bench with a frown on his face.

"That bad, huh?" I say, closing the laptop.

"Hmm? Oh, no. Not bad. At all. It's just…" Mouse looks at me, pained. "This was written from your experience. It was inspired by us. By…me. And how I didn't love you well enough. I made you hurt like that." Mouse's voice breaks and he hangs his head.

"Mouse… I was so young, and so insecure. I didn't know why you did it. I was so confused, that you wanted to break up, but keep being friends. I had all these emotions, and no closure until a few hours ago. You have to understand how much I loved you. I loved you so much, Mouse. And I did not put everything I felt into this character. Not all of the pain she feels is mine. Not all of this pain is because of you. I've dated since you, and he… wasn't the greatest boyfriend either. It's not all about you, not all from you."

"Yes, but some of it is. Some of it has to be; you don't write that eloquently about pain without having felt something that hurt like that. And the thought that I caused you even a small fraction of the pain this girl feels, that kills me. It makes me hate myself."

"Mouse…" I touch his arm. "Mouse, no. Don't…I should be thanking you. Because all of that pain? I didn't just sit with it boiling inside of me. I used it. You hurt me, and I figured out a way to work with the heartbreak. Not around, but through. I made something so good that it might even get published. So, thank you. And please, no more hating yourself. You've gotten so much better since you left, Mouse." I smile encouragingly.

Mouse scoffs. "I was such a wreck when

I left. For weeks. God, I never left my room, I...You used your pain. I let it fester. I turned into this person I didn't recognize. I was so completely different. It scared me. I wasn't myself without you, and since I had no idea how long it would be until I would see you again, if I ever saw you again, I needed to figure out how to get better. And I just felt like you didn't deserve this messy monster of a person I had become, and I couldn't let myself be good again until I set you free."

Tears were starting to spill out of my eyes. "M—Abbot." I laughed and sniffed. "Your eyes...they're so much clearer, now, you know? Like, they were cloudy before. Stormy. Like, I could tell there was so much hurt and sadness behind them. But they're so bright now. Like the skies have cleared."

Mouse smiles without his teeth. "Yeah, I'm feeling a whole lot better these days."

"I'm glad, Mouse. I'm so glad."

He smiles more broadly. "Thank you for sharing your book with me."

"Thanks for not hating it."

"I couldn't ever hate anything that came from you, Sunshine." He dabbed the tears on my cheeks away with the cuff of his sweater sleeve. "Not ever."

I lifted my hand and held Mouse's wrist. I looked into his clear blue eyes, and I feel something growing in me, which feels scarily familiar to the way I felt on the day I officially fell in love with him.

Mouse loved Kelly Sue. He was lost in her. Whenever we went to his house and into his room, his eyes would always linger for a while on his guitar, sitting in its stand in the corner. He'd smile the tiniest bit; you'd miss it if you weren't looking at the right moment. And a part of me, a stupid silly seventeen year old part, was strangely jealous of the way he looked at her. I wanted Mouse to look at me like that. With relief. Like he was home.

The night of the talent show Mouse had secretly signed us up for, he sat in a corner of the black box, tuning his guitar and going over the chords. I was sitting in a chair near the whiteboard, listening to "Landslide" over and over on my iPod.

After the eighth time, I took my earbuds out of my ears one by one, and my eyes fell on Mouse. Because that was always what I did, when I finished doing something. He was like that thing gymnasts and ballet dancers look at to keep their balance. He was my spotting point.

Mouse was playing a Mountain Goats songs I'd watched him learn a few days ago while I read *Pride and Prejudice* for Literature class. He was bent over the instrument, concentration creased into his brow, and that lost look in his cloudy blues.

As he finished the song he sat still for a moment. He ran his hand along Kelly Sue's side, and lifted his head. He saw me looking at him and stood up straight. He blinked slowly. And I knew that, when he opened his eyes again, the lost look would have disappeared.

But then he opened his eyes. And that look? It was still there. Not only was that look, that lost, passionate look still in his eyes, but it was magnified. He was glowing. He looked tired but happy, so, so happy. So happy to be home. And in that little moment that nobody was aware of but us, I was his home.

And as if I wasn't already coming apart inside, his eye-crinkling, life-ruining, blue ribbon smile took over all of his face. That right then was the moment I knew that I was in love with Abbot Wilson Jennings.

The glorious moment was over when he looked away from me, at the stage manager saying something to him. I was so out of my element that I couldn't hear him. It wasn't until our eye contact broke that I realized that I had stopped breathing. I took a long, shaky breath and slumped into my seat.

Later that night, after the show, we

walked a few blocks away from the school to get ice cream in celebration of the uproarious applause and standing ovation, in some cases, that we were given after our performance. We couldn't hold hands because of the bowls and spoons in our hands, so my arm was looped through his instead.

"Hey, do you remember that time like half an hour ago, where we played a version of 'Landslide' that would make Stevie Nicks quake with jealousy?" Mouse said.

"I'm totally okay with the world remembering me only for those wonderful five minutes." I said, spooning out a bite of strawberry ice cream and eating it.

"Oh mirror in the sky, what is love…" Mouse sang.

I thought about telling him I loved him then. The way he looked at me, I was pretty sure he loved me, too. But I was scared, because saying something that raw and vulnerable is scary. So I just scooped more ice cream into my mouth.

"Can I sail through the changing ocean tides...." Mouse hummed under his breath as he scraped melting vanilla from the sides of his plastic bowl with his bright green plastic spoon.

I decided to try again. "Hey, Mouse?"

"Yeah, Sunshine?"

"I..." My mouth went dry. "Never mind."

Save for belting the odd Fleetwood Mac lyric into the empty sky, we were quiet on the walk back to the parking lot, where Mrs. Jennings's car waited for us. We tossed our empty bowl into the trash can of a Panda Express that was on the way back.

We were freezing by the time we reached the car. We both hadn't taken jackets with us, and it was around forty degrees. We got in the car so quickly that Mouse didn't even think to open my door for me. Which was fine, obviously. It was a little too old-fashioned for my tastes anyway. Mouse put the key in the ignition and turned on the heat immediately. We sat in the parking lot while we waited for the car to warm up. I rubbed my hands together and wrinkled my cold nose.

It was silent for a long while as the heat ran.

Mouse took a careful breath before he said to me as he looked through the windshield, "So, you know I love you, right?"

I stopped blowing air on my hands and stared at him. "What?"

"I love you." He turned to me. "Like, kind of more than anything else. More than everything I do, I love you."

I kept staring.

"Is…is that okay?"

And then I was climbing awkwardly over the glove compartment into his lap, taking his cold face in my cold hands and kissing him on his chapped, cold lips. I broke away and stared at this new face, this face of a boy who loved me. And I smiled.

"So, is that a yes?" he whispered.

"Yes, it's a yes. It's okay. It's more than okay, it's…I love you, too."

Mouse smiled the smile that made me crazy and kissed me again. We kissed until our lips were numb and the windows were all fogged up, and it was twenty minutes past my curfew of 10:00 on school nights.

So anyway. Mouse's fingers are touching my cheek and I feel things and it is bad. Really bad. But not bad enough for me to let go of his wrist and move away. It probably actually is that bad, and I'm just so stupid that I don't care about the flowers blooming in the pit of my stomach.

People always talk about getting butterflies when they fell in love. But with Mouse, it never felt like that. It felt like he was the sun, and he was making something from me, something I didn't even know was there, grow into something big and beautiful. Something I never could have grown on my own. And feeling like that again, right *now*, is a terrifying concept. Even more terrifying, though, is the thought of letting whatever had grown die as soon as I let go of him. So I decide to ignore my better judgment for the time being. I decide to just look at him, and feel the petals unfurl inside of me.

Not ever, he'd said. Softly, his sweater on my cheek, his eyes on mine, lost in me.

A screaming child scuttles past us, breaking the moment. We become aware of ourselves, and put some distance between us on the bench. Mouse clears his throat and rubs his neck.

"So, um…" He taps his feet on the linoleum. "Do you want to play another song?"

Another song meant Mouse's guitar and his singing voice. Both very dangerous things right now.

"Um. No." I say. "I don't think... No. That's a bad idea. Right now."

"A bad idea." Mouse nods in understanding. "Sure. Yeah. We'll uh…" He trails off and looks around. There's not much to look at; I know he's just trying to look at anything but me. I know this because I'm doing the same thing.

I try to drown the flowers I've grown in my stomach.

Chapter Sixteen

The weekend after the talent show, it was abnormally warm and sunny for January. Of course by warm, I mean above forty degrees. Mouse and I were on a date of sorts, wandering through the one hundred acre park that was located downtown. He had his guitar, because obviously, and we were walking across the bridge over the Little Spokane River, spouting off the titles of our favorite Mountain Goats songs.

"'Transcendental Youth'," said Mouse.

" 'Marduk T-Shirt Men's Room Incident'," I said.

"Really? That song's such a downer."

"But it's beautiful."

"I'll give you that. Um…." He tried coming up with another one "'Original Air-Blue Gown'."

"'Lakeside View Apartments Suite'."

"'Damn These Vampires'."

"'Never Quite Free.'."

"'New Chevrolet In Flames'."

"'Love Love Love'."

"That song's amazing."

"I know. It's one of the best songs he's ever written. And I think, the best love song ever."

"Really?"

"Yeah. It's just so passionate. So delicate. So good."

"You think so?"

"Yup. If anyone ever played me that song, I would fall in love with them on the spot."

"It's that easy to win your affections? I guess I should learn to sing it then."

"You've already got my affections. But playing that song for me would probably make it impossible to ever love anyone else but you."

"Now I definitely have to learn it."

Except he never did. Finals were coming up, and then we were both caught up in new work for second semester. Eventually he forgot, and I did, too. But I didn't love him any less.

I wonder if forgetting a person and ceasing to love a person are mutually exclusive or not. I guess if you really love someone you never could forget them. But if that's true, I don't know how I ever managed to stop loving Mouse. It must have been that I was so angry with him for the way he ended our relationship that I fell out of love with him. But I don't remember a moment when I thought about Mouse and said to myself "I don't love that person anymore". I always just say to myself that I loved him. Past tense. Saying that I didn't love him anymore felt cruel, an insult to the memory of him, even though the past tense of love essentially meant the same thing. And sure, he'd hurt me, but I could never do or say something to hurt him, even if he wasn't there to hear me. Even if I wasn't sure if saying that I didn't love him anymore would hurt him, I didn't want to risk it. So I only ever used past tense.

I get up from the bench and go the bathroom on the other side of the wall. I wipe the dying makeup from my face and splash cold water on it. I look at my reflection for a minute. My eyes have bags underneath them and my hair hangs limply down my back and shoulders. I find a hair tie in my bag and twist it once around my hair into a big messy ponytail. I sigh at myself and leave the bathroom, and start walking down the corridor, pulling my phone out of my pocket and dialing my best friend's number.

"What is wrong with you, lady? You know it's one in the morning here," Juniper grumbles when she picks up the phone after one ring.

"Oh, shit. Sorry."

"Where are you? Aren't you home yet?"

"No, I'm stuck in Denver. All the flights are offline. Weather stuff."

"And you're bored, so you're calling me?"

"I'm not calling you because I'm bored, June. I'm calling because… somebody I know is here and they're making me crazy."

"What? Who's there?"

"…"

"Oh my God, is it Sandy? If it's Sandy I will personally fly there to tell her off."

"No, no, it isn't Sandy." Sandy was my roommate in college. She was kind of notoriously awful. I wasn't supposed to be stuck with her because I was a junior and she was a freshman, but Housing never helped me solve it, so I practically lived in June's room for a year. Hence the whole best friends thing.

"Then who is it, Sunshine?"

"You know that boyfriend I had in high school."

"Mouse?"

"Yeah. He's um. He's here, too."

"WHAT?"

I jump and hold the phone at arm's length. "God, Juniper, my *ear*."

"*Sorry*. But *him*?"

"Yeah. Mouse."

"Is that a good thing or a bad thing?"

"Yes."

"What?"

"My sentiments exactly. I've been on a rollercoaster of confusion since I saw him."

"Hm." June sounds awake now. "Tell me more."

"He's doing a lot better. And he's ugh,

so effing hot, and so sweet and so… good at smiling." Just thinking about it, I could feel dimples appear in my cheeks.

"Mmm-hmmm."

"I read him the prologue."

Juniper gasps. "Did he hate you?"

"No, he hated himself for making me feel that sad."

"That's too sweet. Where's he living now?"

"Portland. He works at Powell's Books."

"No friggin' way."

"Yeah. And he plays his guitar still. He's gotten really good at it, actually. Well. He was already good."

"You're falling for him again, aren't you."

"Ugh, yes!" I slump against a wall. "So hard. Stop me."

"Is there a shower somewhere in that airport? If so, take a cold one. And avoid him."

"No showers. I can't avoid him; he's literally down the corridor from me. Plus I've already walked away from him three times."

"Why did you keep going back?"

"The first two times, I didn't want to leave us on bad terms. The second time, he came after me. And I was glad that he did. Juniper, what do I do?"

"Well, let's consider your options, shall we?"

I stop walking and sit on a bench. I sigh. "Okay. One: walk away and don't go back."

"Pros?"

"I don't have to deal with him anymore."

"Cons?"

"I don't have to deal with him anymore," I groan and rub my hand across my face.

"Okay… What's Option Two?"

"Option Two…I go back and hang out with him?"

"So, pros?"

"I'm not lonely."

"Cons?"

"I'll probably fall in love with him."

"Is that really so bad?"

"He lives in Portland, Juniper. That's halfway across the country."

"Your point?"

"I just got a call from my boss that my plot has been accepted for the publishing contest. I have to stay in Chicago and write. And why are we just assuming that he's into me, too? That's so narcissistic."

"He wouldn't be hanging out with you so much if he just wanted to be friends. And you wouldn't be hanging out with him if you didn't want that, too," Juniper points out.

"This is so stupid. I'm just tired and bored. I need to sleep. Spending any more time with Mouse is just going to make my life difficult."

"Well then ditch him, Sunshine. You don't owe the guy anything. You need to worry about your own wellbeing, not about if your ex is gonna get butthurt that you're not spending the night entire with him. Get some rest. Forget about Mouse."

"Are you sure?"

"Sunny, what do you want me to talk you out of? Tell me, and I will talk you out of it."

"Talk me out of doing whatever will hurt me the most."

"Don't go back, Sunshine. It might be good now, but come tomorrow, all you'll feel will be pain. Leave it be."

I take a long shaky breath. "Right. You're right. Thank you."

"You're welcome. I'm going to back to sleep now."

"Yes, do that. Sorry I woke you up."

"Don't be sorry. Go find someplace quiet. Just wait it out. You'll be out of there soon."

"Goodnight, June."

"Night, Sunshine."

I hang up the phone and push myself off of the wall. I walk in the direction that doesn't lead to Mouse, and I fight the urge to look back.

Chapter Seventeen

I'm in a section of the airport I've never been in, probably the only part I haven't been in before. It's quiet, with three stores across from me, a coffee place, a tiny bookstore, and a currency exchange place all locked up. The departure board on the opposite wall says the same words it has said all day long.

I lie across three plastic chairs, with my coat bunched up under my head as a makeshift pillow. I'm reading my book again, but the words are bleeding on the page, running together, going fuzzy. I'm too tired and distracted to be reading. But I keep flipping the pages as if I understand what they're saying. I fall asleep with the book dangling from my hand.

The week Mouse and his family moved away, we did something we had never done before every day. On Monday, Mouse went into Boo Radley's—a quirky store with quirky merchandise like bacon flavored toothpaste, Star Trek lunchboxes, and fake tampons that actually held alcohol in tiny plastic tubes—and actually bought something. He'd gone in numerous times, but just never left with anything. He got a horse mask at my behest, and when we got home he put it on and danced around his kitchen. He was a terrible dancer, and the sad thing was, I don't think he was trying to suck. It was wonderful, whatever it was he was doing.

On Tuesday, Mouse and I went swimming at the Y. It was me who had never done that, since my family didn't have a membership card. But Mouse's did, so we used it one last time before the membership got cancelled. I went down the lazy river twelve times, and Mouse and I kissed underwater when there weren't any little kids around to rat us out.

Wednesday, we went to Cold Stone Creamery and ordered humongous waffle cones piled high with huge scoops of all the ice cream flavors we had never had before. Some of the flavor combinations were a little weird, but ice cream was ice cream.

On Thursday night, we climbed on the top of Mouse's roof to watch a meteor shower. Mouse made us both hot chocolate, and he told me all of his secrets.

"When I was a kid, I jumped out of my treehouse to the ground ten feet below. I cut my chin because I landed on a sharp rock. I needed eight stitches," he told me.

"Oh, so that's what this is?" I asked pressing my thumb to the nasty scar on his chin I had always been curious about.

"Yup. When it healed, I tried again, with the goal of landing on my feet this time. My little sister Gloria ran to tell my mom, but when she got back I was already on the ground. Standing up, with this dumb smirk on my face. I thought I was so cool." He smiled and shook his head.

"You showed them, didn't you?"

"Yeah, I showed them what a little shit I was."

"You aren't a little shit," I said.

"I said 'was'. I'm more of an asshole these days."

"You're not one of those, either. You're fantastic."

"So love is blind," he said, with a sigh. He leaned over and kissed the top of my head anyway.

"Tell me another secret, Shakespeare," I requested.

"No, your turn. You tell me something."

"*Me*?"

"You think I just give away my secrets for free?"

"To me? Yes, I do."

"Tell me one. Just one," he begged.

I laughed. "Okay, um…I never threw away my Barbie dolls. They're in a box on the top shelf of my closet. Sometimes, when I'm bored, I take them out, and almost play with them."

Mouse snorted at me. "Almost? What do you just stare at them, fighting the urge to act out some soap opera romance between Barbie and Ken?"

"That is exactly what I do, thank you very much. There, okay? Two secrets. Your turn again. It better be good."

Mouse stared at me for a second. "I want to run away with you."

I blinked. "What?"

He turned his body to face me. "You wanted another secret? That's my secret. That night I came to your house after I found out we were moving, after I cried myself out, I lay in your bed, plotting our escape. I knew it wasn't going to happen, I was just trying to convince myself that I would be okay. That we'd be okay."

"We are gonna be okay, Mouse. I'm not going anywhere."

He smiled a watery smile. "But I am."

"Only physically."

Mouse choked out a laugh and rubbed his nose on his sleeve.

"Right?" I asked.

"Yeah," he said softly. He lowered his head and lifted his mug to his lips.

"So, you gonna tell me this grand plan or what?"

Mouse lay back against the blanket we had thrown across the shingles. "You really want to know?"

"Of course."

"Do you want the realistic version or the stupid version?"

"Um..." I lay with him. "Stupid, then realistic."

"So I steal a horse to drive one of those

pioneer carriage things. I build it myself, and rig it with a sick sound system. In the middle of the night, I go to your house, pack up all of your stuff while you're sleeping, and then wake you up and tell you we're going on an adventure. You get up, and we get in the carriage, but only after you put on all of your clothes at once because there wouldn't have been enough room otherwise. You don't feel embarrassed because I had to do the same thing. We ride off and build a modest log cabin in the middle of nowhere, and nobody ever finds us."

The fact that Mouse was unpredictable had never been more true. "I see."

"I told you it was stupid."

"You did," I said slowly. "What, um… what's the realistic version?"

Mouse wrinkled his nose. "I ask you if you want to run away, you say yes, we leave both our parents notes explaining the situation, take your mom's old car and just drive. We get tired, and rent a room at a sketchy motel. You try to fall asleep from your position of little spoon despite the leaky ceiling and the overbearing terror of not knowing what will happen to us in the morning. I stay awake all night because I'm fucking scared, but not as scared as I would be if I had to live a life where I didn't get to hold you like I'm holding you.

"In the morning, we buy grocery store fruit medley for breakfast, and you take the first driving shift because I'm too tired to get behind the wheel. We drive all day and sit on the hood of the car with cheeseburgers to watch the sunset. When we end up someplace we wouldn't mind living, we find a hotel and make a plan for how to survive the next month."

"Then what?"

"Then we freak out and probably fight because we don't know what to do, and we don't know where we are, and after we both storm off in different directions, we come back together, and I apologize first because I know you won't, and we kiss and make up and get back in the car and go back home, and I resign to the horrible life I'm going to start living that does not include you and your wonderful everything."

I frown. "That's a little more realistic than I was expecting."

"There's no happy ending to this, Sunshine," Mouse whispered.

"Okay, you have to stop saying that. You can't believe that and not want to break up. Either we break up or we make it work. And I love you, Abbot, but if you don't really have faith in this, in us, I don't think we should do this anymore."

Mouse looked in the opposite direction and didn't answer.

"It's up to you, Mouse." I put down my half-full mug of hot cocoa. "I'll let you sleep on it. I'm cold and tired, so I'm gonna go home and go to bed." I kiss his cheek before crawling down from the roof. "Call me when you've made up your mind."

I was laying wide awake in my bed when my phone vibrated from under my pillow, where I kept it at night. Mouse's name was on the screen, below the word CALLING. I accepted the call.

"Hello?"

"Sunshine?"

"I'm here."

"Talk to me. Tell me what you're feeling right now. Make me understand."

I started crying. "Is it really that hard to understand?"

"Tell me, Sunshine. Please."

I covered my eyes and sighed. "I don't know, it feels like…like you're already gone. You feel so far away from me right now, Mouse. It's like you don't believe in me."

"No. *No*, that isn't it at all. I don't

believe in *me*. I don't believe I'm strong enough to last an entire year without you."

"You wouldn't be *without* me, Mouse. We don't have to be in the same place to be together."

"I know, but God, is it easier that way."

"Love isn't always easy, Mouse. Fighting for love isn't ever easy."

Mouse didn't say anything back.

"It wouldn't be the worst thing in the world." I sniff and smooth my bedspread. "We can have Skype dates, and we can text, and I'll send you care packages and letters. We can still text and email. And we can think about all of the amazing things we'll do when we're in the same place again."

"…What would be in these care packages?"

"Um…cookies. Mix CDs. Stuffed animals your friends will laugh at you for, to which you will reply by saying that you are secure in your masculinity as you set them on your bed with pride."

"I like how you assume I'll have friends."

"I'm not sending any plush toys to you until you make friends, Mouse."

"Then I will be sure to make friends with the first person I meet."

"You better," I say with a soft laugh.

"Hey, Sunshine?"

"Yeah, Mouse?"

"I'm sorry. I was being stupid."

"No, you were being scared."

"Anyway. I don't want you to think I don't love you. Because I do. A whole lot."

"I love you too," I said through my tears.

"And I want this to work as much as you do."

"Really?" I turned my head on my satin pillowcase to look at the little picture of him on the corkboard on the wall right next to my bed. He smiled his blue ribbon smile at me.

"Yes. And I'm gonna try. I'm gonna fight for you, Sunshine." He was crying, too. "I'll wait for you until the stars fall outta the sky."

"I'll wait for you until the universe collapses in on itself in an orangey-red inferno," I countered.

"I'll wait for you until…until time itself no longer exists."

"Oh, you will?" I yawned.

"Damn right, I will."

I chuckled sleepily.

"I love you," Mouse said quietly.

"I love you."

"I'll see you tomorrow, okay? We can go out breakfast together. We haven't ever done that."

Tomorrow was Friday, the last full day Mouse would live in Spokane. He and his family would be spending most of the day packing and stuff, so I wouldn't get to see him much.

"That sounds good. Will I see you again before you go?"

"On Saturday morning, before we leave."

"Before that?"

"I don't know; I think my parents want me around all day to help finish up packing and cleaning the house and whatever. If I get even five minutes of spare time, though, I'll bike over to your house and spend the remaining three minutes making out with you."

"God, you better."

He laughed softly. "How do you feel about Cinnabon?"

"Great. I feel great about Cinnabon."

"Wonderful. I'll see you at ten."

"I'll see you first."

"No, you won't I'm very good at blending into crowds. You are horrible at it."

"There's no crowds at the mall on a Saturday morning."

"We shall see. Goodnight, Sun Friend."

"Sweet dreams, Modest Mouse." I hung up the phone and put it under my pillow. I closed my eyes and fell asleep with Mouse's voice still ringing in my ears.

We both had huge cinnamon rolls for breakfast and walked around the mall for a while before Mouse had to go back home and pack. He was busy the entire day, and hardly had time to text me. I spent the day cleaning my own room and working on a project that was due on the first day of the new school year.

All day long, the only thing I could think of doing was walking to Mouse's house and kidnapping him. I would take him for a long car trip or to a movie or out for lunch, or something. It was so unfair to me that he had to spend his very last day here stuck inside his house, putting the life he'd gotten used to in boxes and leaving all of the good things behind.

He texted me once about how he asked his dad if he could take a break for lunch to come see me. His dad had said that he could eat in his room while he finished cleaning it, and that if he wanted to have free time he should have started packing sooner. The problem with that was that Mouse had been packing whenever he had time for the better part of the week, and his dad had only gotten the boxes down a few days ago. His dad was keeping him from me, he said.

I'd never really gotten the chance to meet Mouse's parents. He introduced them to me once when we were on our way out the door. Of course, I'd seen them a few times since then, but not anything long enough to form a sold opinion about them, or for them to form one about me. But from Mouse said about his father, he didn't seem like the greatest person. And I trusted Mouse.

That night I was staying up late reading because all I could do when I tried to sleep was think of him. When I read I just imagined him as a character. It started to detract from the story, so I put the book away.

After half an hour of entertaining the idea of walking to Mouse's house in the middle of the night, I put on my Chucks and grabbed my phone and keys to do just that.

I want you like this. I want to spend all of tonight with you, Sunshine.

I want you until the sun comes up.

His blue ribbon smile. Our shirts on the floor.

Mouse's hands explored my torso and all of the skin he hadn't ever seen before. There was something on his mouth. Not his face-breaking smile, but something softer. Like a gentle reverence. He pressed his thumbs against my rib cage. I straddled his hips, pushing my heels against the small of his back until he came closer to me. Our lips kept almost touching, like two magnets centimeters away from each other, but not actually snapping together.

I finally gave in to the ache to kiss him, doing so deeply and tugging on his bottom lip just the tiniest bit. We'd never gone so far as this, and now that we were, all of the stops were pulled. All of the things I had wanted to do with him, I finally let myself do.

I mussed up his curls, and I unhooked my bra and put his hands where I knew he wanted them to be, and I ran my fingertips just below the waistband of his jeans. Mouse shivered and sighed. I pushed him back against the pillows and unbuckled his belt and yanked his jeans off. He shook out of them and pushed them off the bed. Then he gathered me in his arms and flipped over so I was on the mattress. Mouse pulled the covers up from where they had been at the end of his bed and ducked underneath them.

I could feel his warm lips all over my chest and stomach. My hands gripped the sheets when he kissed my hip bone, just above the top of my jeans.

Mouse pushed back the blankets and gasped for air.

"Hey," he said.

"Hi," I said in a high voice.

"How you doing?"

"Great. How are you?"

"Awesome. Can I take off your pants?"

"Go for it."

"Cool." Mouse disappeared back under the covers.

I could feel his fingers unbutton and unzip my jeans. I lifted up my hips so he could pull them off, and tried to remember what underwear I was wearing and if it was cute. Purple polka-dotted hipsters, I remembered. Good. Not embarrassing.

Mouse came back up and settled softly on top of me, propping himself up on his arms. He smiled with his eyes.

"You're so beautiful, Sunshine," he whispered.

I broke our eye contact. "Thank you." I ran my hands up and down his back, my fingernails softly scraping his skin.

He rested his forehead on mine and kissed me. I held his face in my hands and pushed short, fast kisses onto his mouth until my lips were tired.

Mouse slid down below the blankets again and left a line of kisses down the middle of my torso, from the middle of my breasts to the waistband of my hipsters. His lips lingered there, and I felt his hands on my hips, and his fingers hooking underneath the lace on the top, and then out again, unsure of himself. I lifted my hips up again, inviting him to remove them, and he did.

In the morning—later in the morning—I woke up before Mouse did. I lay on my side and watched him sleep. He was splayed out on his stomach in the queen-sized bed, his face smushed against his pillow, his mouth half open and his lips thick with sleep. I put my finger in his hand, and he gripped it like a baby. I lifted his arm and got underneath it, draping it over my stomach as I snuggled up to him. His breath teased a tendril of my hair. It occurred to me then that unlike me, Mouse didn't have satin pillowcases (although he should have. His hair would be less dry if he did) so my hair was a giant horrible mess that would take hours to untangle.

I pushed my hair back over my shoulders and brushed my cheek against his.

"Abbot Wilson Jennings," I said softly. "I love you. I'll love you no matter where you go. I will love you as long as you smile the way that you smile, and as long as you say my name the wonderful way that you do. I'll love you for as long as your eyes shine and your shoulders relax when you see me. For as long, and for as far, as either of us care to go."

One of Mouse's eyes cracked open.

I felt myself blush. "Shit. You weren't supposed to hear that. I thought you were asleep. Did you hear that?"

"Every word," he answered, his voice soft and slow.

I groaned, and he laughed and kissed me cheek.

"Is it really that embarrassing?" he asked me.

I nodded, squeezing my eyes shut. "The most embarrassing."

Mouse chuckled. "You are forgetting that I've seen you naked."

I opened my eyes again. "I refuse to feel embarrassed about my body."

"As well you shouldn't," Mouse said, smiling gently. "That thing—the embarrassing thing you said—it sounded like goodbye. Were you going to leave before I woke up?"

"I shouldn't stay. What if your parents came in?"

"They don't come down here."

"Well, what if my parents wake up and find out that I'm missing?"

"They'll assume that you're doing what all teenagers do in the morning during summer vacation and sleeping in," he answered. "Besides, what are they gonna do if they find out you're with me? Say you can't see me again?"

I understood what he meant. It was a little late to ground me from Mouse.

"Yeah…" I said and felt all of the gears that make me worry slow to a stop.

Mouse regarded me for a short second before saying, "Don't feel like I'm forcing you to stay, or anything, though. You can go."

I thought about it again for a second. Only a second, because any longer would set those gears back to work. By way of replying, I leaned into him and kissed his sleepy mouth. He sighed and kissed me back.

I rolled on top of him and kissed him again, then his chin and his Adam's apple, which bobbed up and down as he yawned. His warm arms came around me, his hands slowly wandering over my sides and hips and breasts, and my body rose against him with every deep breath he took. I kissed him again, and my hands brushed through his wiry Mouse-brown hair, and everything happened like it had before, except slower and easier, and we stayed together like that until dawn broke and sun fell onto us through his window.

After it all, we lay there, he on his back, and I on my stomach. He fell asleep again. I got up and dressed quietly so he wouldn't wake up. I stood by his dresser while I tied my hair back and noticed a pile of guitar picks. I picked one of them up, and left one of my earrings there in its place, a la *The Breakfast Club*. I saw a notebook on the top of an open cardboard box, and tore a corner of paper from it and scribbled him a tiny love note.

I couldn't stop thinking about this poem when we were together.

> Maîtresse, embrasse-moi, baise-moi, serre-moi,
> Haleine contre haleine, échauffe-moi la vie,
> Mille et mille baisers donne-moi je te prie,
> Amour veut tout sans nombre, amour n'a point de loi.

Tout mon amour,

Soleil

I looked at him one long last time, locking away this morning in a vault in my head, where only the best thoughts and memories lived. I remembered his bare shoulders and back. And his clothes strewn over his otherwise clean floor, and I remembered the way he'd said my name last night, his eyes squeezed closed, his hands holding mine so tight, the way he sighed and gasped and groaned, and the way he had made me do the same.

I walked up the basement stairs and out the back door right next to them, thanking the powers that be for not letting anyone see me leave my boyfriend's house at six thirty in the morning.

Chapter Eighteen

This airport is horrendously boring when nobody is hanging out with me. I'd invite anybody's company at this point. But then I realize that I'd be a total drag because I'm tired and depressed and my heart isn't happy with me. I'd probably end up spouting off the entire story of Mouse and I to any unsuspecting person who happened along my path, the way I had with Laura the Bartender.

I just decide to try and fall asleep again.

(Mouse)

I miss her. I realize that I probably shouldn't miss her, but I do. In fact, this entire night all I've been able to think about is how much I have missed Sunshine. Breaking up with her was like breaking off a piece of my heart. No, it wasn't just my heart. It was all of me. I broke off a piece of me when I broke with her, and it hurt like hell for a long time, but I guess at some point I'd just gotten used to the pain.

Because right now, I remember it. I remember it, and I feel it. It's excruciating. Death probably wouldn't hurt as much. This thought had occurred to me more times than I would like to admit after Sunshine stopped talking to me. I never tried, though. I knew Sunshine would kill me if I did.

I didn't kill myself, but I did fall back into my old ways. Angry and anxious, and lonely. I'd made friends before I broke up with her, and after we stopped talking, I never hung out with them anymore. All I did was hole myself up in my room. I didn't even sleep. Everything was so scary without her. Everything was so dark without Sunshine.

She said she was going to the bathroom, but that was almost an hour ago. She probably ran off again. She'd already done that a few times already. It hurts more and more each time.

I shouldn't let it hurt. Why am I giving her permission to hurt me? I shouldn't let this person who had been absent in my life for years shouldn't be hurting me as much as she is.

I'm reminded of the first night I was away from her. It hurt like this. I wanted it to hurt then. I needed to remember her existence. It hurt because she was real, and so far, but she still loved me. I let her hurt me then because I had to make myself remember Sunshine, that there was someone as wonderful as her in the world. It hurt because I loved her, and she was missing from me.

But right now it shouldn't hurt like that. And yet, it does. I miss her. I would say she was missing from me except she isn't mine to be missing from anymore.

I think about going after her, but that's probably the last thing she wants. She obviously didn't come back for a reason. I wish I knew what I did wrong. I wish I could make it better between us. She's worth fixing things for.

She's so bright and smart. I can't believe how far she's come since I saw her last. When I left, she was a seventeen year old girl who loved telling the story behind everything. Now she's twenty-two, and steps away from having her own book published.

And here I am, at twenty-one, working in a bookshop and living with a group of people I can barely tolerate. I mean, I love Powell's but I never thought to myself once in my life "I want to be a bookseller when I grow up." I wanted to write songs. I used to do it all the time. I tried to write Sunshine a song once, but it sounded too much like an Elliott Smith song so I scrapped it and never tried again.

I did learn "Love Love Love" for her, though. It's a Mountain Goat's song she always said was the most passionate love song in the world. I never got the chance to play it for her.

I was gonna play it over Skype for her. I'd sang to her that way before, but the last time I did, we both ended up crying. It was kind of a sad song, with lyrics that went *I miss your face like hell*.

When I broke up with Sunshine, it was a few weeks until Christmas. All of the carols and the decoration and couples being all cute was totally depressing me. I tried to rectify it by Skyping her while we both drank cocoa and watched *Miracle on 34th Street*. When the movie was over, we imagined being together on a real date. We hypothetically drank eggnog and ice-skated, and rode in a horse-drawn sleigh, and slow danced to "Happy Xmas" and kissed under mistletoe. But it just wasn't the same. There was this slow, pining ache ringing through my body the entire time.

When I fell asleep that night, I dreamt that we were together, doing all of the things we'd wanted to do for Christmas. When my little sister woke me up for school, it felt like such a cruel thing, taking me out of the imaginary place where I got to be with the girl I loved.

For a few days, I was at war with myself over it all. What if there was some guy at school that she met, who was cuter than me, or better at talking about feelings than me, or was just better because he was there and I wasn't. What if she wanted to do all those romantic Christmas things for real, with a real, live, present person who liked her? I should let her have that, I thought. I wanted Sunshine to be happy, not miserable because she felt guilty about doing anything because her weird, sad boyfriend lives in Wisconsin and she can't cheat on him because she knows it would wreck him.

But what about waiting? That was what we said we were going to do. We were going to pick a university to go to together. We had already started looking at New York University,

University of Chicago, a couple of state schools, and Stanford, even though only Sunshine had even the slightest chance of getting in. It was almost January, and then only a few months until graduation, and then summer, and we would be together again. It wasn't that long, I kept telling myself. Sunshine was worth the wait.

And I was pretty sure of myself for a good weekend, until my dad brought Sunshine up at dinner.

"So, I never asked," he'd said. "How did Sunshine take it when you two broke up?"

I set down my fork. "We didn't."

"What?"

"Sunshine and I didn't break up."

"You didn't? Why not?"

"We decided we're going to go to the same college."

"College is a few months down the road, Mouse."

"I know."

"You're gonna make that girl wait for you until September?"

"It was her idea, Dad." I poked around my steamed broccoli.

"And you didn't try to talk her out of it."

"Why would I talk my girlfriend out of not breaking up with me?" I asked, exasperated, dropping my fork on a plate with a loud *clink*.

"Abbot," my mom said. "Please."

"I'm just saying, isn't it a little selfish of you to keep her waiting like that? What if she meets someone else, what if she gets bored or lonely? Do you really want to hurt Sunshine like that?" my dad said.

"I'm not hurting her," I said. My voice broke.

"You're keeping her locked up like a bird," he said accusingly.

"I'm not." I looked down at my lap.

"Abbot, think about it. Think of Sunshine. You love her, don't you?"

"*Yes.*"

"Then let her go. Set her free, Mouse. It's for the best. For Sunshine *and* for you. You need to be present. Your mind is still in Washington. Wisconsin is your home now."

But that wasn't true. Sunshine was my home. And being away from home was tearing me apart.

But that doubt my dad had seeded in my mind took root, and soon I knew what I had to do.

We usually Skyped every night, but I knew I wouldn't be able to say what I needed to say to her face. So I emailed her instead.

So I know I'm supposed to call you, but tonight isn't a great night for that, so I thought I would email you instead.

I think we should break up.

I'm sorry.

Mouse

It was the hardest email I ever wrote. I wanted to explain myself, but it all felt like excuses, so I just wrote what I needed to say, and sent it before I could change my mind. I got an email back a few hours later.

But the stars are still in the sky.

After reading that message, I couldn't reply right away because the tears in my eyes made it impossible to read the keys on the keyboard. I went to bed and replied in the morning.

I can't see the stars. It's raining here.

She sent something back a few hours later, saying something like "Oh. Okay" and I sent something like "So how's school?" or something stupid like that. Talking to her again so quickly was one of the biggest mistakes I have ever made, I realize now.

That, and never playing her that song.

I haven't played it in years. I wonder if I can remember how it goes.

Chapter Nineteen

I wake up disoriented at one in the morning. I sit up, and find that my neck is sore from me sleeping on it funny. I stretch my arms up over my head and get up. Craving even the simplest form of human interaction, I start wandering around again, people watching, walking with nowhere to go.

As I walk I get this horribly annoying little jolt of excitement whenever I see a curly haired guy in a cardigan. It is, of course, never who I think it. It isn't ever Mouse. It's never who I am hoping it will be.

No. Not hoping. Expecting.

I don't care about Mouse Jennings. I do not. Care. About him. At all.

God, I wish the restaurants would open again already. I'm starving.

I remember that I have a muffin in my bag from a long time ago. I find a table to sit at and withdraw it from my purse. It's in its little brown paper Starbucks bag, still, which is much better than the alternative muffin crumbs littering the bottom of my old cross-body tote. I open the paper bag and take out the muffin. It's a little bit squashed and crumbly, and it tastes stale, but it is food, and I am desperate. McDonald's is open, but I already ate their once tonight, and when it comes to eating McDonald's at the airport, once is more than enough.

I press the tiny streusel crumbs left on the paper on my fingertip, and lick them off. I notice out of the corner of my eye another lanky guy in a cardigan; he's even got a guitar case this time. I know it's not him, and for a good twenty seconds I don't look up to make sure.

When I do look, I'm surprised. Because it *is* Mouse. I almost call him over but I snap my mouth shut just in time.

(Mouse)

I can feel someone's eyes boring into the back of my head. I try to ignore it and focus on the departure board. Not much change. I turn my head to look out the window. The snow has let up a good amount. Flights could start coming online soon. Which is fantastic news. I don't think I can stand much more of this place. Like Sunshine said earlier, it's like Purgatory. Neither here not there.

Okay, this staring person is making me anxious. I swivel on my heel to stare back at them, and nearly trip over my own feet when I recognize said staring person as Sunshine.

I gape at her for a good, long moment.

I nearly take a step closer, but the I remember that she's avoiding me, and think better of it. Sunshine blinks at me. I smile awkwardly and wave. She waves back slowly, then beckons me over to the table where she is sitting.

"Did you follow me here?" she asks suspiciously.

"What? No. I've figured out by now that you want nothing to do with me." I say, folding my arms on the table top.

"How'd you manage that?"

"Well, you ditched me three times. I put two and two together."

"Mm. So how are you?"

"Exhausted and bored. And how are you, Sunshine?"

"Oh, you know. About the same." She crumples something made of paper in her hand. "I… I don't know if I'm sorry or not. About all the ditching. I keep thinking it's a bad idea for us to be hanging out, and then we always end up in the same place again."

"I'm not asking you to be sorry, Sunshine. Would you like me to go?"

Sunshine thinks for a minute. "If you do, we're bound to cross paths again. Might as well save time and just stay in the same place."

"Okay. Whatever you want."

Sunshine nods slowly, and looks down at the table .Behind her glasses, her glasses have dark circles underneath them, and are a little red.

But I'm with her again. And it makes me feel so good. It feels like home.

Which of course it shouldn't. Because it's been too long. Too long without her. But that fact that it's been so long makes it better. It's deeper this way, somehow.

I'm home. And I love her.

I lay my head on my folded arms and bask in the Sun.

Chapter Twenty

Mouse is looking at me weird. His eyes are dilated, dreamy and tired. His face is pale, and his mouth is curved into this weary smile. Like some nomad glad to have a warm bed at the end of the day.

Cautiously, I slide my hand across the tabletop. Mouse unfolds one of his arms, and reaches it out until it meets mine. Our fingers mesh together and I am alarmed how well they still fit together. I feel safe this way, his fingers pressing gently against all of mine. I set my chin on my folded arm like Mouse and smile softly at him.

This is so dangerous. But I don't care.

Later in the morning of the day Mouse and his family were to drive to Wisconsin, I drove to his house to say goodbye. There was a huge moving truck outside his driveway, and their garage door was open. I parked on the other side of the street and got out. I could see Mouse in the window of the living room. He flashed a grin at me and moments later he was bounding down the steps of his front porch and running across the lawn to me. He hugged me.

"You still managed to leave without saying goodbye," he said, brushing my hair out of my eye lashes.

"Only because you fell back asleep. Did you find my note?"

Mouse turns splotchy. "Yes," he mumbled. "I had to punch it into Google Translate. But wow."

"Wasn't that just a little better than a goodbye?" I asked in a low voice.

"Only in some respects."

"Really?"

"It would have been hotter if you'd said it to me and not written it."

"Yes, but then I would have to go to the

trouble of translating and that would have just been distracting."

"I would have been too busy being overcome by how inexplicably hot it was that you'd just spoken French to me in my bed while things not involving clothes were going on."

"Whatever." I kissed him.

Mouse broke away and looked at me. "In all honesty, though…wow."

I smiled at him.

Mouse took my hand. "Come on. We aren't leaving for another half-hour. Mom and Dad forgot something they need for the trip and so Dad ran out to the store." Mouse took my hand and led me into his house. We sidestepped a mover and I waved to his mom, who was on the phone with someone. She smiled and waved back. We went down the stairs to the basement.

Mouse's bed was gone, along with all of the boxes that were in his room the night before.

"Wow," I said.

"Yup," Mouse said as we slide down the wall and sit on the carpeted floor. "Kind of depressing, isn't it?"

"Yeah, kind of." I could see the holes from the thumbtacks that used to hold posters that wallpapered Mouse's room in the opposite wall. "I can't believe this. It's all so real now."

"I know," he whispered.

I curled into him, putting my head on his shoulder. Mouse put his arm around me and my head slid down to his chest. "Fuck," he said softly. He squeezed his eyes closed and let his head fall against the wall. "*Fuuuck.*"

I sighed and sat quietly for a minute.

"Hey," I said, tilting up my head to look at him. I reached and put my hand on the side of his face. He opened his eyes and looked down at me sadly. I pulled him down to me and touched my lips to his.

Mouse twisted around and pulled me into him. He kissed me harder, and it felt the way kisses soldiers would give their wives before they went off to war in documentaries looked.

I leaned away from him so I could breathe. Mouse's eyes, open now, were cloudy and sad. His hand moved up and held the back of my head.

"Hey," I said softly.

"Hi."

"Are you okay?"

Mouse took a long breath in. "I don't know."

"Can I help?" I rubbed his shoulder.

"Distract me."

I sat up and brought Mouse's head down to my shoulder. I traced patterns on his back and sang "Moon River" quietly. Mouse gave a hiccupping sob on the line *wherever you're goin', I'm goin' your way.*

I kissed his neck when I finished singing. "Only a year, Mouse. We can do a year."

"A year without the sun," he reflected. "The world wouldn't last five minutes without the sun."

I swallow and sigh. "I am not the sun. Just like you're not a mouse. I do not have control the weather or the world. I only have control over myself. And I love you, Abbot. I love you endlessly. But I really don't want to be the deciding factor in whether or not your world crashes down when you move away."

Mouse pulled away and stared at me with red-rimmed eyes.

"I'm sorry," I said quietly.

"No. Don't be sorry." His hand brushed my cheek. "I'm putting too much pressure on this. On us. And on you. I shouldn't have done that. I'm sorry. I love you."

I smiled with relief. "I love you, too."

Mouse kissed me.

"I don't want you to think I won't miss you, though," I said. "Because I will. Like a shit ton. But I love you more than I'll miss you."

Mouse smiled sadly back at me, but he didn't say anything back.

We didn't speak to each other again until we stood outside of his car, while his parents finished double-checked everything they could think of, and Mouse's baby sisters, Gloria and Laney ran around in the yard, doing childish things, as children do.

"I love you," Mouse said to me. "You are beautiful and wonderful and I will text you all day long and call you when we get to the hotel."

"Good."

"And I will call you every day. Maybe more than once some days."

"You are more than welcome to do that."

"And I love you."

"I love you, too."

A crease appeared in Mouse's forehead. I smoothed it with my thumb.

"Don't worry, sweet boy. This isn't goodbye. This is just a little chapter. A year is nothing in the grand scheme of things. It'll fly by, and then we won't ever have to worry about having to do this again."

Mouse nodded. "I know," he said. Then, with more confidence, "I know."

"Mouse!" Mrs. Jennings called from across the yard. "Load up Gloria and Laney, will you please?"

"Yeah, Mom," Mouse said. "Just a second." Mouse jogged after his sisters. "Hey, Gloria! Laney, get down from there! You're gonna fall on your face. I speak from experience."

I laughed as Mouse tried to grab his wriggling sister from a tree branch a few feet above his head. I wondered how she got up there. She was tiny and only five years old. Gloria ran past them to the car. She looked up at me.

"Mouse really likes you," she said.

"He does?"

"Yup. He talks about you a whole bunch. And his skin gets all funny when I call you his girlfriend."

"Yeah, it does that." I looked around to make sure he wasn't watching, then leaned down to whisper. "It's a little icky looking, isn't it?"

Gloria nods. "It's like a rash."

I snorted. "Yeah. A little." Of course I didn't mention how I kissed all the red patches on his neck and chest hours earlier.

"Anyways, thank you for loving my big brother. You make him really happy. He gets really sad when he thinks 'bout how he's not gonna see you again."

"He will, Gloria. We're gonna go to college together."

"What's that? Mom and Dad keep saying that word to Mouse and I don't know what it means."

"It's like far-away school where really big kids go live by themselves and learn about what they want to do when they grow up."

"Ohh," Gloria nodded with understanding. "And you and my big brother are gonna live together at college?"

"Well, we'll at least be at the same one."

"That's good. I don't think he'd be very good at taking care of himself."

"You don't?"

"No. Sometimes he forgets to eat. And sometimes he sleeps all day."

"Hey, what are my favorite ladies talking about?" Mouse came back with Laney tossed across his shoulder.

"You." Gloria said frankly.

Mouse swung Laney down into his arms and strapped her into her car seat. "What about me?"

"It's a secret," Gloria and I said at the same time. I winked at her. Gloria tried winking back, but she just blinked really fast.

"Oh. Okay. Come on, Gloria, Mom and Dad want you guys in the car."

"I have to talk to Sunshine. Cover your ears, Mouse," Gloria said.

Mouse slapped his hands over his ears and hummed. Gloria crooked her finger at me. I bent my knees so we were at eye level.

"You promise to take good care of him in college, right?"

"Yeah. Will you take good care of him before then for me?"

"I'll try."

"Pinky promise?" I held out my pinky.

Gloria linked her little finger with mine. I gave our hands a shake.

"Good. So long, Gloria."

"Bye-bye, Sunshine." Gloria clambered into her car seat.

Mouse uncovered his ears and strapped her in. He closed the car door.

"What was all that about?" he asked me.

"Oh, she's just looking out for her big brother," I explained.

"Ah."

"She's sweet. I wish I had a sister." It was only me and my older brother Sébastien.

"Careful what you wish for."

"Mouse! We're leaving in five minutes!" Mr. Jennings shouted from inside the house.

"Okay!" He shouted back. He looked at me, and I expected his eyes to be panicked. But he looked at peace. "Thank you for the most wonderful nine months of my life. I never would have gotten this far without your help."

I stepped closer and put my hand on his waist. "You made me braver. Do you know that?"

Mouse's blue ribbon grin spread across his face. I traced all of the creases and curves it created. I stood on my toes and kissed his smile. Mouse hugged me close, and lifted me off my feet. I tried to memorize everything about this moment. His chest and the way it raised and lowered with every one of his breaths. The sweet summer air. His arms, and the strength in them I always underestimated. His mouth and his lips, drawing a kiss out of me that could last him a year.

I touched him in all of my favorite places. His hair and his hands and his back and his ears and cheeks and his neck. All of the places that I could touch in front of his sisters without feeling weird.

We kissed shamelessly until his parents

came outside and his mom got in the passenger seat. When Mouse's dad turned the car on, Mouse reluctantly pulled away.

"I love you," he said breathlessly.

"I love you."

"I'll call you tonight."

"I'll answer."

"I love you."

"I *love you*."

"I love you too."

"Mouse!" his dad yelled.

"You gotta go," I said, backing away.

Mouse nodded. He walked to the other side of the car and got inside. He bent over so he could look out Gloria's window at me. He waved. I waved back. Then I waved to everyone else. The car backed up and drove away.

Mouse was looking back at me until they

turned the corner.

A seconds later, so got a text message from him.

le Soleil est partout

The Sun is everywhere.

Chapter Twenty-one

We move from the little table to a bench in a different part of the airport. It's one we've been in before; I think it's even the same bench. We're sitting sideways on the bench, thumb wrestling. Mouse is winning by one point.

"So, what would you do if you weren't working at Powell's?" I ask as my thumb evades his.

"I would be out of a job," he says, pulling our arms toward him.

"No, I mean, what would you do instead?"

"A different job."

"Mouse."

"Fine. I'd…I'd write songs. That's what I want to do."

"What kind of songwriting? Lyrics, composing?"

"I'd really like to try it all. But I'm much better at composition than writing. You remember."

I catch his thumb underneath mine. "Ha-ha!" I shout victoriously.

"Ow ow ow let go let go." Mouse winces.

I release his thumb. Mouse shakes his hand. "Jesus, Sunshine what's with the death grip?" He sticks his thumb in his mouth.

"Sorry. God."

"It's fine. We're tied now, anyway." He pulls his sweater sleeves over his hands.

"So, what's keeping you?" I ask.

"What?"

"From songwriting. What's keeping you from doing it? It's what you want to do, isn't it?"

"I'm not *not* doing it. I just…haven't tried selling any of them. It's a hard business to break into."

"Why don't you start a band?"

"I tried once. It didn't work out. Ended sort of horribly, actually."

"Why didn't you tell me about your band when I asked about your and your music earlier?"

"You asked if I was still doing the music thing. And that particular music thing I wasn't doing anymore."

"What happened?"

"I had to move."

"What? Why?"

Mouse sits silently for a moment. Like he's guilty of something.

"Why did you have to move?"

"Because I was dating the lead singer. And living with them."

"You've dated since we broke up?"

"Just the one. Does that matter?"

"I guess not." I wait a moment before asking my next question. "What was her name?"

"Alex."

"Hmm."

"Short for Alexander."

"What? You dated a guy. Wait, are you *gay?*"

"What? No."

"Oh."

"I'm bisexual," he says, like he had it rehearsed.

"*Oh.*"

"Yeah," he nods at his lap. "I was going to tell my family at Christmas, but after seeing how they reacted to Gloria being a lesbian, I thought better of it. I did tell her though. She needed my support in that way, I think." After a beat, he asks carefully, "It doesn't bother you, does it?"

"What? No. Not at all. It's just…how long have you known?"

"A couple of years. In college. I kissed one of my friends on a dare, and I decided that kissing boys is just as awesome as kissing girls."

"I see."

"Nothing happened with the guy, though. The college guy. He was just simultaneously heterosexual and secure in his masculinity."

"A rare combination these days." I say, shaking my head.

"Tell me about it."

"So which one broke up first?" I ask.

"Out of what?"

"The band or you and Alex?"

"Oh, Alex and I broke up first. He broke up with me. My insensitivity was apparently a lot worse than I thought. And then the band broke up a few days later. It wasn't a big deal. We never did anything but play at coffee shops and sometimes the Portland Saturday Market."

"How long were you together?"

"Alex and I were together for ten months. I moved in after five. The band was together for about a year."

"How long ago was that?"

"A year now, I think."

"Sweet."

"Oh, that reminds me. I almost forgot to…" Mouse takes a little device out of pocket and pricks his finger on the pointy tip sticking out from the top.

"To what?" I ask as I watch him.

After a moment, he looks up from the device at me and says, "I need to change my insulin pump."

"Oh. How do you do that?"

Mouse lifts up a corner of his shirt to reveal a discreet white pod attached to his side. "Just gotta switch this guy out for a new one. I'll just be a minute. Watch my guitar for me?"

He opens his guitar case, moves Kelly Sue and opens the compartment underneath her. He takes out a little carrying case and goes to the bathroom.

As I wait for him, I wonder how he found out he had diabetes. And when. Was it before or after we broke up? How did he handle it? How different is his life now? He asks as if it isn't but I know that's not true. Disease changes people, as hard as we try not to let it.

Mouse comes back a few minutes later and puts the case away. I shake the heaviness of my thoughts off my shoulders.

"Sorry about that," he says, sitting down again.

"Hey, gotta stay alive." I smile at him and push my glasses up my nose.

"Yeah, living is a good thing to not stop doing at this age."

"So, what did you just go do? Sorry, I'm just curious."

"No, it's fine. I just had to fill a new pump with insulin, take off the old one, and put the new one on. I should probably eat something, but I kind of forgot to grab something for later when the shops were still open."

"Oh." I feel guilty about my muffin now.

"I'll be fine, though. It's not a big deal. I'll hit up a vending machine if it comes to that."

"M'kay." I say. "Hey, do you maybe wanna play some more songs?"

"I thought you didn't want me to play Kelly Sue again."

"Maybe I changed my mind." I raise my eyebrows.

Mouse studies me. "Okay, then. What should I play?"

I shrug. "Surprise me."

Mouse gets his guitar out. "Okay." He tosses the strap over his shoulder and takes a pick from his pocket. He starts strumming and softly singing Elliott Smith's "Between the Bars". I start singing with him. Watching him play now feels more intimate than it had before. It takes me a minute to realize that it's because Mouse is actually looking at me while he's singing. The eye contact is so rare and intense that I can't help but hold it.

When he finishes playing he is still looking at me.

"Hi," he says.

"Hi. You sounded good."

"Thanks. You did, too. Should I play something else?"

"Sure. Do you have something in mind?"

"Yeah, if it's okay with you."

"Go for it." I sit back against the bench.

He starts playing. *Pluck, pluck, pluck, strum. Pluck, pluck, pluck, strum.* My throat goes dry when I recognize the song. He starts singing.

And now I'm back on the floor of his old bedroom, neglecting my Chemistry homework and singing while Mouse slowly plays. I'm holding his face in my hands and kissing his eyes and cheeks and nose. I can almost hear him say "I think I'm falling in love with you."

As he plinks out the last few notes, I find that I'm on the verge of tears.

Mouse sets Kelly Sue aside. "Are you okay?"

I swallow the lump in my throat. "Yeah. Yeah. I'm just going to go to the bathroom really quick. I'll be right back."

I jump up and practically run to the nearest restroom. It's a private one, without stalls, so I don't worry about containing myself. As soon as the door closes, I let the tears fall. I slide down the door and drop my head into my hands. I shake with body-wracking sobs, bigger and harder than I knew I had in me. I must be overtired, along with overemotional.

The way Mouse singing that song affects me can only mean one thing, and it scares the living shit out of me.

I tip my head back and swallow. My throat aches. I close my eyes and all of the wonderful moments Mouse and I ever shared start flashing through my mind, and with "Moon River" stuck in my head, it's like a movie montage. It starts with him draped with Broncos memorabilia, and ends with him saying, "I couldn't ever hate anything that came from you, Sunshine. Not ever."

I can't feel this way. I CAN'T. I try to convince myself by listing off the reasons in my brain.

1. He's so different

2. *I'm* so different

3. I have to focus on work now more

than ever, leaving no time for a relationship.

4. I don't even know for sure that he feels the same way.

5. I'm going places, and following my dream.

6. Mouse needs to figure himself out.

7. I live in Chicago.

8. And he lives in Portland.

9. So I'll never see him again.

10. Even if he did like me, too, long distance clearly doesn't work for us.

11. I should be okay with moving on. This shouldn't affect me like this.

I can't love him, I tell myself. I'm not allowed to.

"God, get it together Sunshine." I say

aloud, my voice rough and strained.

I rub my hands over my eyes and wipe away the wet remnants of my mascara. I stand up and unwind a length of toilet paper to wipe my eyes and blow my nose.

I look at myself in the mirror, and take deep breaths.

"You are not allowed to love him." I say firmly.

(Mouse)

She'll come back. She said she would be back. I repeat these words to myself when it has been three minutes since Sunshine went to the bathroom.

I pick up Kelly Sue again to distract myself. I strum an E, followed by an A. And I find out that I still remember that song.

I start singing it quietly to myself, watching my fingers as I play, trying to shut out the rest of the world. I finish one verse, and I can vaguely hear someone walking to me, and I know it's her. She stands a few feet away for a while, but I don't look up. I only sing the second verse a little louder.

Halfway through it, she decides to sit down. She draws her knees into her chest and rests her forehead on top of them.

I keep singing, and each word is deliberate. Every chord, every note, every breath is for her.

I only look at her for a moment, as I sing *"Then we shall see each other face to face."* But her head is still down, so I look away again.

It's a hard song to sing, I realize. It's passionate, like she said. It makes me feel vulnerable. It almost feels too intimate to be doing here and now, but something deep inside me demands that I keep singing.

I can feel the emotions that playing this song evokes start to become present in my throat, and then in my voice. I swallow whatever it is that hurts so much before singing the last two lines of the verse.

The song ends with a final strum, and I let out a long sigh. Sunshine finally looks up at me; her eyes are red and dripping with tears. She looks shattered.

"Sunshine," I say with the weak voice I've been left with.

She swallows and unfolds her legs. She jumps up from the bench. I put down my guitar immediately. She backs away from me, stumbling as if she's wounded, and with one final look, she runs away.

Chapter Twenty-two

Fuck, I think as I listen to his voice sing the song I never thought that he would.

I'm in love with him.

He finishes playing and I look at him. Only to find that he is already looking at me.

He says my name: "Sunshine", in the sort of voice someone would have before a first drink of water after being stranded in the desert. Like he had been lost at sea, and I was the first dry land he'd seen in days.

Like a prisoner of war seeing the sun for the first time in weeks.

And all of my biggest fears have suddenly become true.

Tears drip down my red-hot face. They started falling again as soon as I sat down and dared to listen to his song. I gulp the swollen lump in my throat that came from holding back sobs, and then I get up from the bench, looking at him one second longer, before running away again.

Again.

I love him, I think to myself as I sprint through the crowds, my heart pounding in my ears, tears and snot running down my face.

I fell in love with Mouse, even though I promised myself that I wouldn't. I fell in love with the way he smiled and the way he said my name. I fell in love with the way that nothing had changed, and the way that nothing was the same.

I want to pinpoint exactly when I fell in love again, but I can't. It was this slow, sinfully easy progression. I loved him, I loved him, I loved him, I love him. *So stupid*, I chant to myself in my head. It syncs up with my heartbeat. *So stupid, so stupid, so stupid.*

And so scared. *God*, Mouse.

I was running away, but all I wanted to do

was run back. I want to run back to him, and ask him, just to be absolutely sure that he meant the words he was singing.

But doing that would just make everything worse. Because I know Mouse. I know he wouldn't sing that song if he didn't mean it. And knowing that he means it, and being with him at the same time is a recipe for disaster.

I've been running longer than I've ever had to run since high school. I stop for a second, doubling over to catch my breath. I need to hide myself. I need to cry again.

Why do I love that stupid boy? All he does is make me cry.

I stand up straight and recognize the section of the airport I'm in. I remember there's a restroom around the corner. I jog to it, and ignore all the people inside, locking myself into the handicapped stall and letting it all come out.

I half expect one of the ladies to come ask what's wrong. Thank God they don't they all leave after a minute or so, and I'm free to cry louder.

Jesus Christ, Mouse. *Mouse.*

Mouse and his hands. And his sweater and his hair. And his eyes, and his bow legs and his new strength. Mouse and his smile and his guitar. Mouse. And his name and his voice and the way he walks and how he never gave up on me. Mouse and Mouse and Mouse.

All this time since we've been together he's been fighting to be with me. To share this tiny sliver of his life with the girl whose heart he broke a lifetime ago. I hope he doesn't give up on me now. I'm reckless now. I'm reckless for him.

And so completely terrified.

I curl up on my side, and hide my face in my arms. I never thought I would spend so much time crying in the bathrooms today. Mouse,, ruuining everything.

Mouse, taking my heart. And me, letting him.

(Mouse)

I'm almost certain she won't come back this time. God, I'm an idiot.

I sigh, and chide myself. I lost her. Worse, I think I hurt her, too. I'd tried to hard not to, but I did. Why do I always break her? What kind of monster am I to keep breaking the sun?

I put Kelly Sue away and slide down on the bench until I'm lying down. I scrub my hands over my face and try to think of what to do next.

I could go after her. But I don't think she wants that.

I could call her. If I had her number. But I don't.

I could do absolutely nothing. I could just lie here and wait for my flight to come back online. And then I could get on it and fly home and try to forget all of tonight. I think remembering it would hurt more than any of the pain associated with Sunshine so far.

But I want to see her again. I need to see her face. I want her here with me. We wouldn't even have to talk. But I'd want to. I'd want to tell her how I feel. How I've never really stopped feeling that way.

Loving Sunshine Ballanger is like breathing, exactly like it. I have always done it, sometimes without even thinking. Stopping for too long would kill me. It would burn and I would fade and then I would just stop living. If I stopped loving her everything else would stop, too. It's terrifying to think about, but not at all is it untrue.

I need to see her face again. So I do, the only way I can without hurting her again.

I watch her videos. On my phone, I pick up where I left off, and then just start watching whichever ones look good from the Recommended tab.

She's hilarious in all of them, without even trying. She just talks for a while, and then there's this perfect pause before a punchline, and then she'll say it and I bite my lip to keep from laughing aloud. Her timing is flawless, effortless. Like everything that she does.

I watch her have this life I didn't get to be a part of. I watch a tour of her tiny apartment, and I watch her talk about the books she's read. I note the small changes in her physical appearance. She's not wearing makeup in one, her hair is up in another. It looks even more like wool than it did before. I told her that it did, once, and she compared me to Hannibal Lecter.

It's a long story.

God, I miss her. It's been, what? I look at my watch. Half an hour. It's two in the morning. I'm completely past the point of being tired. I play another video and pretend that she's really here, because this is as good as it gets.

Chapter Twenty-three

I've stopped crying and now I'm just slumped against the wall of the bathroom stall. I don't know what to do next.

But none of what I want to do is what I should do. Doing what I want has only gotten me into trouble so far tonight. Now here I am: Cold, sad and tired, hiding in the bathroom from the boy that I love.

He's not a boy anymore, I remind myself. He must be twenty-one or twenty-two now. Old enough to drink and vote and do whatever else he wants. Mouse is a man.

I pull out my phone to distract myself. I check Instagram, and favorite a few tweets. I scroll mindlessly through Facebook. I watch a video one of my friends linked to from YouTube. And then I'm on YouTube, watching some new videos by other BookTubers about Christmas book hauls or whatever. I watch a vlog, and a new episode of a webseries that I like.

I go over to my channel and check the comments of a video I put up a few weeks ago. I reply to a few, and close down the app when I come across some troll putting in his two-cents about my boobs.

I haven't made a new video in a while. I should probably do that. Yet another thing to do when I get back home.

I wonder if Mouse subscribed to me. God, what if he watched my old videos? I remember him saying that he's watched most of them, so he's probably seen the bad ones, too. They were all so horrible in 2012. Bad lighting, a crappy Flip camera, and I was still trying to get the hang of editing. Also I was just sort of horrible at talking to the camera when I started. I said a bunch of embarrassing things.

I could make a video now, I think to myself. My iPhone is charged. I wouldn't be able to do much in the way of editing, but I'm too tired to get into the editing process anyway.

But what would I talk about? I can only

think about one thing. One person. Maybe getting all my thoughts out would help. I could always delete the video later.

Maybe Mouse will find it, and then I'll feel like less of a jerk for just up and leaving the way that I did. Making a video would at least give me a chance to explain myself, if only a little.

I prop my phone up on the toilet paper dispenser as a makeshift tripod, turn on the camera, and start recording.

(Mouse)

There's a new video on Sunshine's channel. It looks like a book review, as it's titled "Of Mice and Men". The background of the thumbnail is a tiled wall I think I've seen before. I tap on the video to play it.

Sunshine looks tired. Her face is drawn and her eyes are glassy. She takes a long breath.

"So I should probably tell you now that this isn't a book review of *Of Mice and Men*. Sorry. I know the title is kind of misleading. This is more of a…vloggish type thing. I'm probably going to delete it soon."

She rubs her hands over her face and sighs. She looks away from the camera for a second.

"There's a mouse outside. I saw it while I was…and I freaked out. I probably should have done something with it, but I just ran off. And locked myself in the bathroom.

"I should go out and find it. Right?

But…it could be anywhere. And what am I supposed to do with it when I find it, *if* I find it, then what? Do I pick it up…do I…? Do I take it home? I can't take it home, he's got his own stuff to figure out.

"And I can't kill it. Because it's…"

She looks down.

"He's just so good. You know? He's so…smart. And he's been so nice. And I told myself I wouldn't…" she groans and pulls her hair. "I need to stay away from him. I can't go out and find him. I need to let Mouse go home. We have our own lives now. Our pasts don't matter."

Except that they do. At least a little bit.

"Or…I don't know. If we didn't have a past, there wouldn't be any problem with Mouse being outside someplace. If we didn't have a past, I probably wouldn't even notice him. He wouldn't have noticed me…

"I'm sorry. I'm sorry, this is so stupid. I can't believe I'm making this video. He probably isn't even watching it. I'll delete this soon. I'll make a better video later this week."

The screen goes black for a second. Then she's back.

"But if he was watching. He could find me if he wanted. Not…that it matters anymore."

She sighs and reaches forward to turn the camera off.

And then it's over.

I could find her. But I have no idea where she is. Well, I know that she's in a bathroom. But which one? There's a million of them in this place.

And it's not like I could go into it, unless it's a unisex one.

She did go in one a few hours ago. I was waiting for her outside of…someplace.

I gather up all of my shit and go in search of a directory. I find one, and count sixteen unisex bathrooms on the map, all at different wings of the airport.

    I start with the closest one. I probably look a little bit crazy, running through the airport with a guitar case on my back, but I could not care less at this point. I just want to find her. I have to talk to her. I have to see her. Actually see her.

Chapter Twenty-four

I regret putting up the video almost as soon as I hit Upload. My thumb hovers over the delete button, but at the last second, I think better of it. I'll delete it tomorrow. When this, whatever happens, will all be over.

Regardless of what happens, there will be crying. As there's been already. I've never cried like this in front of Mouse. By some unusual standard, Mouse was always the crying one in our relationship. I don't think Mouse saw me cry more than once.

That one time it had to do with the fact that he smoked and I hated it. He wasn't addicted or anything, but sometimes he just lit one up. To calm down, sometimes. Or because he was bored. He could make a pack last for weeks. But I didn't like that he had a pack at all.

The first time I found out was one night when I was cold and he dropped his jacket (leather, gorgeous on him) on my shoulders. I stuck my hands in my pocket, and the left one curled around a little box. I took it out and raised my eyebrows at him.

"You smoke?" I asked.

"Not regularly," he said with a guilty look on his face.

"But you smoke."

"Sometimes."

"*Ew*. Why?"

Mouse shrugged. "Mostly as a distraction. When I need it."

"And how often do you need to be distracted, exactly?"

"God, I don't know. I live a sort of stressful life."

"Yeah, so do I. And I manage not to need to smoke."

"I'm not you, though, am I?"

I scowled, put the pack back in the pocket I had found it in, and crossed my arms.

"I'm sorry if you don't like it," he said after a stretch of tense silence. "I promise I'm not addicted. I don't have black lungs. It's just to calm me down. I know it's gross."

"Good. Because it super is."

"Try not to hate me, okay?" He took my hand and kissed it.

I smiled in spite of myself. "It would take more than the occasional cigarette for me to hate you."

"I'm glad."

I really actually only saw him smoke once. He was waiting for me to come over. I found him lying on his back porch, staring up at the cloudy sky, with a cigarette between two of his fingers. He put it to his lips, and took a draw from it, and then blew a gray wisp into the sky. It was actually kind of hot, but I wasn't ever going to tell him that. He might start doing it more, and I had no desire for our kisses to start tasting like ash. Or for him to die of cancer.

"You look like a greaser," I said after a minute of watching him.

He lifted his head and looked at me. "I look like a what?"

"A greaser. You know, like those gangs members in the 50's or whatever with the duck-tail hair and the rolled up pants and leather jackets. They smoked and had rumbles and snapped their fingers a lot. Iconic greasers include Ponyboy Curtis and Danny Zuko."

"Thank you, Wikipedia." Mouse clambered to his feet, dropping the cigarette onto a patch of dirt and stomping it out.

"Won't your parents see it and ground you or something?"

"Nah. My dad smokes. They'll just assume it's his."

"Oh."

"Yeah. Anyway, hi." He walked towards me and leaned forward to kiss me. I stepped back.

"What's wrong?"

"You smell like smoke. And you're gonna taste like it, too. If you want to kiss me, you're going to have to brush your teeth first."

"Fair enough." Mouse opened the sliding door that led into his house and bounded up the stairs into the bathroom. "I'll even change if you get me a clean shirt," he said as he pulled a blue toothbrush from a cup.

"Okay." I went back downstairs and then into the basement to get a shirt from his room. I found my favorite one of his folded neatly in his top dresser drawer. It was a red and white baseball tee. His collarbone was *made* for baseball tees. I snatched it up and went back upstairs.

"Here," I said, holding out the shirt.

Mouse spit toothpaste into the sink and took it from me. "Thanks."

He pulled the shirt he was wearing off by the collar. I got a fast glimpse of his shirtless self before he put on the clean shirt. I wanted to look longer.

"There," he said. "So can I kiss you now?"

"Yes, you may."

He grinned stupidly and wrapped an arm around my waist. He pressed his face against mine, and our lips found each other, coming together naturally.

"Hey," Mouse said when we broke away, our noses almost touching we were still so close.

"Hi. So, are you ready to show me your expert baking skills?"

"Hell yeah, I am." We head back downstairs to the kitchen. "So…does the smoking actually bother you?"

"It doesn't please me."

"Do you want me to quit? Because I would. If you wanted me to."

"Really?"

"Yeah, I mean, it's not good for me, anyway. And hey, there are other ways to keep calm, aren't there?"

"I'll make you a list." I smiled.

"Deal. So, what do you want to make?"

"What do you know how to make?"

"Muffins, cookies, um…pie. But we don't have pie stuff. Cake, but cake seems like a special occasion food, doesn't it?"

"I think quitting smoking qualifies as a special occasion."

"Not one I want my mom or little sisters to know about when they open the pantry and see a cake with 'Way to kick the habit!' written on it in icing."

"Fair enough."

"I can do pretzels too. But maybe we should check what ingredients are available to us before we go too far. We can go shopping if we need to."

"Grocery shopping. Very couple-y."

"I couldn't agree more."

We ended up making peanut brittle and eating in Mouse's room. We were both lying on our backs, being quiet except for the snap and crunch of the confection we had created.

"You've never been on my bed before," Mouse said.

"Hm," I said swallowing. "You're right. I like it here. It's soft."

"You look good here."

I raised my eyebrows at him.

"Sorry," he winced. "That was creepy."

"I don't care," I said. I rolled closer to him, and lay on my side. Mouse turned his head, and gently chucked me on the chin.

"So what do you worry about that makes you turn to cancer sticks to calm yourself down?" I asked him.

"I don't know. My dad, I guess. And school. Sometimes everything piles up when I turn my back for just a second, and I freak out, and just reach for it."

I frowned.

"It's…maybe not the best thing to turn to," he said.

"Yeah. You know what you could turn to instead?"

"Alcohol?" He smirked.

I rolled my eyes. "No, dumbass. Me. Your friendly neighborhood girlfriend."

Mouse looked up at the ceiling again. "Nah, I don't wanna make you all depressed. They're my problems."

"Mouse, I don't know if I've made this very clear, but I'm sort of invested in you. Your problems *are* my problems. I want to help you with them. I'd feel better if you called me when you were worried or whatever, instead of letting a bunch of leaves wrapped up in paper slowly kill you."

He looked at me again, raising his eyebrows slightly.

"Because I love you and stuff." I mumbled.

"I love you too, Sun friend."

"Enough to let me help you?"

"Enough for that. But…you can't fix me, you know? I've gotta do some of this shit alone."

"I know. I'm just…happy that you'll let me help."

"That means more than you can ever know, Sunshine. I don't think anyone's ever… cared like you do. At least, not as much as you."

"Oh, stop, you'll make me blush," I said, pushing my face deeper into the pillow.

"You don't blush," Mouse said, combing his hand through my hair. "You glow. You beam."

I rolled my eyes.

"But really, thank you," he said. "It means a lot. You mean a lot."

"You mean a lot too, Modest Mouse. Not much in my life means as much as you do."

"You'll make me blush."

"You don't blush. You get splotchy red patches all over your neck."

"I do?"

I nodded. "And sometimes, your ears turn red."

"Hmm."

"You get all red and white. Like

strawberry shortcake."

"That has to be an embellishment."

"It doesn't have to be," I said, and kissed his cheek. "But it is."

"I'm a red, splotchy baby."

"Ugh, don't say it like that. It makes me feel like a pedo."

Things were fine for a long time, and Mouse seemed happy. But one Friday, I only saw him one time at school during passing time. He looked tired and scruffy and angry. I was so surprised that I didn't even say hi.

I called him after school to see what was wrong. And he didn't pick up, which was weird. I decided to walk home the long way, so I had to pass his house.

I was walking past the park when I saw a person leaning against a tree in a leather jacket. The person had curly hair. And red Converse All-

Stars. And a cigarette in his hand.

"MOUSE!" I shouted and ran towards him.

He jumped and turned around. "Shit," I could hear him mumble as he stubbed his stupid killing device on the tree's trunk.

"*Ce que le baiser que tu fais?*" I shrieked, which was French for 'What the fuck are you doing?'

"I'm…" he looked away from me and sighed. He smelled horrible. "I'm sorry."

"That doesn't answer my question."

"Maybe because your question was in French, a language I do not speak."

"I asked what you're doing," I said in a furious monotone.

"Isn't it obvious what I was doing, Sunshine? I was smoking, okay? I broke our promise; I screwed up; I didn't sleep at all last night. I'm sorry."

"Why didn't you talk to me? I told you to talk to me."

"Sunshine."

"Are you sure you're not addicted? Because it certainly seems that way."

"No. I'm. I'm not."

"Then why is it so hard for you to stop?"

"Because I don't want to."

"You said it was gross!"

"Yeah, I did. But so am I."

"Only when you smoke, Mouse."

"Only *all the time*."

"Would you shut up?! This isn't about how fucked up you are. This is about how you promised to come to me when you felt anxious and you lied."

"I never promised that."

"You did. You said you would let me help you. But you didn't. You came here and lit one up instead!"

"Sunshine, I'm sorry."

"You said you loved me enough to let me help you. And you lied."

"No. No, I didn't. I do love you. I want you to help me."

"Then why are you out here, ignoring my calls and avoiding me at school?"

"Because…! Because all you can do to help is talk to me. And talking only works so much."

"I'm not good enough?"

"Not enough to fix it all, no. Helping and fixing are two different things."

"But you can't fix yourself without help, Mouse!"

"You don't know that."

"Yes, I do! You proved it to me when you smoked a cigarette instead of doing something like figuring out why you were upset. You proved it by lying to me. Don't you want to get better?"

"Sunshine, would you stop? You don't even know what problems I have."

"Then tell me, Mouse! Jesus."

"I can't."

"Yes, you can."

"No, Sunshine, I really can't." He tugged at his hair with both hands. "I…can't tell you my problems. And you can't help me with them."

I felt tears start to come up. "Mouse…why?"

"Because I don't even know what they are. I just know that I'm screwed up. And yes, I want to go to therapy to figure out what the hell is wrong with me, but you don't have any idea how opposed to that idea my dad will be. And if my dad doesn't like it, my mom won't either. And the high school counselors can only do so much before they have to talk to my parents."

Tears dripped down my cheeks. "Let me help you find out what's wrong. We can do research, you can schedule a private appointment somehow, I'm sure. You don't have to be alone, Mouse. Please don't isolate yourself with this. It isn't safe."

"Sunshine…I don't want you to…" Mouse swallowed his words and turned away from me.

I sniffed. "Don't want me to what?"

"I don't want you to…I don't want to show you the dark parts of me. I don't want to scare you off with my demons. What if whatever I've got going on inside of me turns me into this monster who isn't worth loving."

I sighed and pressed my gloved hands under my eyes to soak up my tears. "Mouse, that could never happen."

"How can you be so sure? How are you so certain that everything will be okay? I could be crazy. I could be depressed."

"You *are* depressed, Mouse."

"What makes you think that?" he snapped.

"Because…" I took a steadying breath and stared down at my boots. "I know what depression looks like."

"How do you know what depression looks like?"

I folded my arms and tried to shrink myself. "Because I have depression."

"What?" He turned around again. "Why have you never told me?"

"Why haven't you told me about whatever you've got going on inside your head?"

"Okay, so you can keep your demons private, but I can't? That's not fair, Sunshine."

"You don't know, but that doesn't mean nobody does. My parents know, my therapist knows. I have help. I have *welcomed* help. You haven't."

Mouse sighed.

"You're just hurting yourself. Cigarettes might calm you down, but every time you reach for one, it breaks you a little bit more."

"I know," he said quietly.

"You do?"

"Yes. Do you think I like that this is the only way I stay sane?"

"It doesn't have to be that way, Mouse. It really doesn't."

"It's better than other things."

"Like what?"

"You know which other things."

I wasn't quite sure, but I had an idea that it had something to do with self-harm. More…alarming self-harm.

"It's not. Not really. Those thing only kill

you if you let them." I hated saying it.

"It hurts less."

"Does it hurt less than talking to me?"

Mouse shrugged.

"Mouse, I will not love you any less if I know what your demons are. Everybody has them. That doesn't make you worthless. Or loveless."

"You say that now, but what about when you find out what's really going on inside of me? How can you be so sure that I won't scare you off?"

"Because I know my heart better than you know your mind. I don't change so easily, Mouse. Do you really think that I could stop loving you just like that?"

He still wasn't facing me. It hurt.

"Do you really have that little faith in me, Mouse?"

He didn't say anything back.

"Is this really even about me? Or is it about you, and how you'd rather smoke as a form of escapism than face whatever's going on inside of you? Are you scared of your parents finding out you need therapy or are you afraid of going, because you don't know what's wrong with you, and you don't want to know, and you don't want anyone else to? Are you scared of yourself?"

His shoulders slumped, and he dropped his head.

"Mouse? Abbot?"

I took a step towards him and put my hand on his shoulder. He flinched, but didn't move away. I anchored him to me, my arms going around his middle and my forehead resting on the middle of his back.

"Because that I understand."

I felt Mouse turn around, and his arms go around me, hugging me closer to him.

"I'm sorry," he said, his cheek against my hair. "I'm sorry about…everything."

"I forgive you."

"I'll stop. I promise I will. I'll throw them out. I'll do it today."

"Thank you."

"And I'll try counseling. I'll go after school. Okay?"

"Okay. So okay."

He kissed the top of my head. "I have faith in you, Sunshine. I do. You're so wonderful and so good. I don't deserve you."

"Does anyone really deserve anybody?"

"I'm not sure. I'm only sure that you are too wonderful for me."

"And yet here I am," I said, moving my head back to look at him. "Loving you."

"You must be nuts."

"I am," I kissed him on the cheek. "Certifiably."

"There's the explanation I've been looking for." He kissed my lips quickly and took my hand. "Let's go. It's freezing out here."

We walked out of the park and to a coffee shop. Mouse tossed his pack of cigarettes in the first trash can we passed. His shoulders relaxed and he breathed with an air of finality.

And even then, my crying was just a few tears. I don't think I've ever all-out bawled in front of him. I did cry a lot though, on my bad days. I had so many bad days. I still have them, all the time.

Now that I think about it, Mouse probably won't want to try again. I mean, it was him who broke up with me in the first place. Because the distance was too much. He'd never try again, even now that he's happier, or older or whatever. And I don't think I would say yes to the idea of trying again, for the same reasons.

And now hiding from him doesn't make any sense. Or at least, not as much sense as it used to. Especially when all I want to do is be with him.

One night can't hurt, right? We might as well enjoy each other's company while we can. While we're in the same place. Which might not ever happen again.

The thought sends me spiraling into another bout of tears. I may never see Mouse, this boy I love, ever again. I knew falling in love was a stupid idea.

It doesn't feel like it was my idea. I feel almost as if the heart and the mind are two different beings. And my heart took me over, and here I am. I'm so angry at it. My mind is so angry at my heart.

Wouldn't being with him now just make parting ways more painful later? What's the point in being happy now if I know I won't be later?

I'm starting to think that there isn't one.

(Mouse)

I've checked fourteen of the unisex bathrooms. Every time it was awkward. And every time Sunshine wasn't there. I'm losing steam and heart, and hope. Where is she?

I check the fifteenth, and she isn't there either. But I stay for a minute to sit down and rest. I'm not feeling very good. I bend over, resting my forehead on my knees, willing myself not to puke. I pass a vending machine, but stopping to buy something and eat it seems like a waste of time.

After a few deep breaths and a drink of water, I force myself to go check the final restroom.

When I get there, it's quiet. Nobody is in here, not that I can see. But there's a handicapped stall at the very end.

"Sunshine?" I say just loud enough to be heard.

I hear a sniffling gasp.

"Sunshine, is that you? It's…Mouse."

"Um…yeah. Hi."

I sighed with relief and slumped against the stall door. "I thought I wouldn't ever see you again."

"You can't see me,"

"I mean… I thought you…I saw your video."

"You did?" she says, sounding tearful. "Oh God, what a mess that was. How did you know which bathroom to go into?"

"I didn't. I took a hunch that you were in a unisex, and I checked all of them."

"Mouse…" she sniffs again. "You shouldn't be here."

"I thought you wanted me to come."

"I did. I…used to."

"And now?"

"And now...I'm so glad you found me. But I don't think that this is a good idea."

"What's not a good idea?" I ask, sliding down to a seat on the floor, leaning back against the wall.

"All of this. Us. Being together."

"Why?" I ask gently.

"Because I—" she chokes on her words.

"Hey, hey, it's okay. Are you okay?"

"I don't know," Sunshine whimpers. "I don't know...anything."

I scoot closer to the door and press my cheek against it. "Hey...don't cry, sweetheart. Please."

She tries to say something, but she's crying too hard.

"Hey, are you sitting by the door?"

"N—no."

"Well, I am. I'm right on the other side. If you sat right next to the door, it would be like sitting together, but you wouldn't have to look at me."

A moment later I hear four footsteps, then see her legs stretch out in front of herself.

"Okay. I'm here."

I put my hand out under the stall door, palm facing up. She hesitates, then sets her hand in mine. I grasp it tight.

"So...I get the idea you don't really want to talk right now. So I will instead. Is that okay?"

"Yes." She sniffles again and sighs.

I lick my lips and stare up at the fluorescent lights. "Sunshine...I feel like should be sorry about something. But the thing is...I'm not. I am not sorry about any of this. I'm not sorry that I saw you by the window, and I am not sorry that I went up and talked to you. I'm not sorry for one minute of the time that I've spent with you. Well. I could have done without the arguments, I guess."

Talking has somehow exhausted me, so I close my eyes and tip my head back and breathe shallow breaths.

"And maybe... maybe I shouldn't have held your hand like I did before, or looked at you the way I did, or played that song. But I did do all of those things. And I don't regret any one of them."

I swallow and sigh. "Look, Sunshine. I know that it's crazy. And that it's been five years, since we were together and only ten hours that we've been in the same place since then. And I know it wouldn't ever work, and I would never dream of trying long-distance again. I would never ask you to make it work. Hell, I don't even know if you give two shits about me at all."

Sunshine gave a coughing sob.

"But...*I love you.* I think there's like this little piece of me that never stopped loving you, and then I saw you again, and that little piece grew, and it grew and it grew until it wasn't just this little piece. It was this entire thing, it was something whole. It was every cell of me, loving every cell of you. And I know that your cells and my cells probably aren't the same ones we had when I kissed you goodbye in my driveway, but they're still me, and they're still you. I was with you and then all of the pieces fell into place. And I love you, and I don't regret it."

Everything is quiet.

"Sunshine?" I say weakly. I think that declaration took whatever energy I had left. "Please say something."

It's quiet for a few more minutes. Then:

"*Va te fair encule.*"

I blink. "What?"

"You speak French. Don't you know what I said?"

"You told me to go fuck myself, didn't you?"

"...*Oui*."

"Um. Why?"

She takes her hand out of mine. "Because, oh my God, Mouse. What the hell am I supposed to with that information?! You can't tell me that kind of shit when your flight to PORTLAND could come back online at any goddamn second. I'm shit at goodbyes as it is, Mouse. You know that. What the hell do you want from me? We can't...you can't..."

I close my eyes, pained. "I know. I know. I'm sorry. I'm so sorry. Sunshine."

"Jesus *God*, Mouse."

"I'm sorry."

"God, why did it have to be now? Now, when we have lives. Good lives. All this potential and opportunity. It's not like I can up and leave now. I can't leave my job and go to Portland to be with you, Mouse."

"I know. And I don't want you to. I just

needed you to know that I love you. Please for the love of God, don't change your life for my sake."

Sunshine sighed. "And God knows what long-distance does to us. It wouldn't be any easier now."

"I know," I say faintly. "It won't be. This isn't me telling you I want to try again. That would be unfair."

I feel like I'm going to faint. I really should have eaten something.

"Telling me you love me isn't fair either…"

And then the world is black and silent.

Chapter Twenty-five

"Because…because I love you, too. And it's unfair that we can't make it work." I pull my fingers through my hair and groan.

It's eerily silent in the bathroom. I was certain Mouse would have something to say to that.

"Mouse?"

He still doesn't say anything. But I can hear him breathing.

"Mouse?" I pull myself up to my feet and unlock the door. I slowly pull it open, and see Mouse sitting—more like slumping—on the floor, against the wall. His eyes are closed.

"Oh my God, Mouse." I drop to my knees in front of him. I put my hands on his face. "Mouse, talk to me."

He is completely unresponsive.

"Mouse, wake up!" I cry. I scramble to my

feet and run out the bathroom door. I run up to the first security guard I see. "I need help. My...there's a man passed out in the bathroom."

"What? Show me."

I lead him to the bathroom where Mouse lies against the wall.

"Were you here when it happened?" he asks, kneeling down and taking Mouse's pulse.

"Yes. Well. I was in one of the stalls, and we were talking and then I said...something and he didn't respond, which was weird because he had been talking, like, two seconds ago. So I opened the door and I saw him like this."

The security dude looks up at me. "Why were you talking to him through a stall?"

"That's... a long story."

The guard sets Mouse's limp arm on the cold floor. "If it wasn't serious he would have woken up by now."

"So it's serious?"

He ignores my question. "Do you know of anything that could have caused this?"

And it dawns on me. "He...he has Type One diabetes."

"I'm calling 911." He stands up and starts muttering into his walkie-talkie.

I kneel next to him and shift him so he is lying down. Then I worry that he could throw up, so I roll him onto his side so he won't choke. I brush his hair out of his face.

"Please be okay, Modest Mouse," I say softly. "I need you to be okay. I need you to know what I said."

He's wearing his guitar across his back, so I carefully slide the strap over his head and set the case down gently on the floor.

"Paramedics will be here soon," the security guy reports. "Do you want me to stay with you?"

"No, thank you. But could you maybe

keep people from coming inside?"

He nodded and went out the door. I bent over so my forehead touched his temple and held his hand.

"Abbot Wilson Jennings, *qu'ai-je fait pour vous?*" What did I do to you?

I stay like that until I feel arms pulling me away. I jump and turn around to see a paramedic with her hands on my shoulders.

"Ma'am, I'm going to need you to give us room to work."

"Oh. Sorry." I move back to sit against the wall and watch them while they work.

"He's diabetic?" one of the other medics asks.

"Type One. He said earlier that he had to change his insulin pump and that he should have eaten something afterwards, but all of the restaurants are closed because it's…" I don't have any idea what time it is. "…late."

"Was he exercising?"

I shrug. "I mean, he's done a lot of walking. He just looked through the entire airport trying to find me."

"And who are you?"

"I'm his..." Saying I'm his ex feels like an oversimplification. But it's the only thing I know for sure. "I'm his ex-girlfriend."

The paramedic who pulled me away says, "Sounds like diabetic hypoglycemia. Do you know what medical supplies he has with him? He might have an injection of glucagon. That would give him the spike in blood sugar he needs."

"Um...he took his insulin thing out of his guitar case. I'll show you."

I unzip Kelly Sue's case and take her out, opening the compartment underneath her. The paramedic searches through it.

"There's only insulin in here," she says.

"Does that mean you have to take him to

the hospital?"

"We would have to, anyway. But yes. He needs medical attention immediately. There's an ambulance at the nearest exit. Would you like to come with?"

"Yes, please." I stand up.

They put Mouse on a stretcher, and I have to look away. He's so lifeless. I keep having to repeat to myself "he's alive; he's not dead; he'll be okay." I force myself to look at him long enough to see his chest move up and down, proof that he's breathing. He's still in there, somewhere.

The security guard has kept any curious passersby at bay, for which I am thankful. I don't know if I can deal with other people right now.

The paramedics tell me to get into the back of the ambulance first, then they load Mouse's stretcher on. I want to hold his hand, but as soon as the doors close, the paramedics swarm him, hooking him up to IVs. They're talking and working, but I'm almost unaware of it. My mind can't focus on anything but my thoughts.

I kept telling myself that Mouse has only changed for good. But this, this disease—it isn't good. I don't know the first thing about diabetes. All I know is that it somehow effects blood sugar. I don't know what's happening to him, and I wouldn't know how to deal with it by myself. If I was the only one around when this happened I might have killed him because I would have had no idea what was happening to him.

After a few minutes, I notice that the medics have sat down, and Mouse is lying in front of me, tubes stuck to his arms, and an oxygen mask over his face. I gasp and start crying again.

"Everything will be all right ma'am. What's your name?" the lady paramedic asks.

"Sunshine," I manage.

"Abbot will be fine, Sunshine."

"How did you know his name?" I ask her.

"We tried asking you, but you were in

shock. We looked at his driver's license."

"Oh." I wipe my eyes on my coat's sleeve. "So what happened to him?"

"When he changed his insulin pump, he should have had something to eat, but he didn't. So he needed a glucose injection, which we gave him. The doctors will monitor him, he should wake up soon. He'll probably stay until later today. Mid-afternoon, I'd guess, so he has time to rest and recover. After making sure he's all taken care of, he will be released into your care."

"My care? But I don't know what he needs."

"Just keep an eye on him."

"But…my flight. I live in Chicago."

"Ah," the lady nods. "He lives in Oregon."

"How do you—?"

"Driver's license."

"Right." I lean back against the metal side

of the ambulance and sigh. "I'm going to stay with him. Until he's out, I mean. I don't even know if the flights are back online yet. Did you see the departure board?"

"There are a few international flights online. The rest should be back online soon. I'm sure they'll let you exchange your tickets, if you haven't already."

"I haven't." The day has been so busy, it never even occurred to me to do so.

"I'm sure he'll be happy to see a familiar face when he wakes up. You said he's your ex?"

I sigh. "Yeah. We were high school sweethearts. But then he moved so we broke up."

"That's tough. My boyfriend went on a two month-long trip last year. It was torture."

"Yeah. It sucked."

"So, have you been with him all day?"

"All night, more like. But yes. For the most part. I did run away a few times."

"But then you came back?"

"Or he found me."

"What kind of guy is he? Aggressive?"

"Mouse, aggressive? No. Not anymore. Never towards me. He wouldn't hurt a fly." I'm just assuming. He doesn't seem like the kind of person to get into fights anymore, especially since he seems to be avoiding things and situations that might turn aggressive, i.e. drinking and bars.

"So if you're broken up, why'd you keep finding each other?"

"I don't know…Because we're in love, I guess."

Then she raises her eyebrows at me.

"He told me, just before he passed out. I got really mad at him, because telling someone something like that when you're both about to fly to different parts of the country seemed kind of cruel to me."

"But you love him, too?"

"Unfortunately."

"Does he know?"

"I don't think so. I think I said it the literal second after he blacked out."

"Are you going to try to tell him again?"

I think about it for a good long time. "I don't think that's a very good idea."

"You don't?"

"Because it will give me hope I can't afford to foster. I don't have the luxury of toying with the idea of being with him. It's just not something I can do."

"What do you have in Chicago that you can't have in Portland?"

"A chance to have a book I write get published."

"Can't you work on it from Portland and send it when it's done?"

"No. It's an elimination process, a real job that I have to be present for. I can't leave Chicago."

"What's Abbot doing in Oregon?"

"He works in a bookstore, he's got roommates. He's got a life. I'm not going to ask him to leave Portland for me. He already said he wouldn't ask me to go to Portland for him. I just need to keep any chance of a relationship between us from happening."

"You don't sound very happy about that," she remarks.

"I'm tired, and stressed and irritated and worried about Mouse. Of course I'm not happy."

"Here," she says, handing me a shock blanket. "I think you need this."

"Thank you." I take it and unfold it, tossing it over my shoulders and cuddling into it.

When we get to the hospital, the

paramedics tell me I have to wait for Mouse outside. They take him behind a set of doors and I sit in the empty waiting room with the shock blanket still around my shoulders.

I have to dissuade Mouse from loving me. Because if I can convince him otherwise, then I won't feel like I have to tell him I feel the same way. I won't feel compelled to make it work.

I know he said he wouldn't dream of doing long-distance again, but when we were in a long-distance relationship, we were high school students with little to no personal income, certainly not enough to fly to see each other frequently. But now that we're adults, we have the power to create some sort of schedule. Every other month, holidays, birthdays. It wouldn't be impossible.

That's what I can't let myself believe. What I can't say to Mouse. I just need him to not love me.

(Mouse)

It's black. And there's this incessant beeping noise. And I don't remember the bathroom floor being so soft. I open my eyes. A nurse is checking my vitals.

"Am I in the… hospital?" I ask groggily.

"Yes, you are."

"Fuck. What did I do to myself?"

"You gave yourself an insulin injection without eating."

"Damn it. I knew that was a bad idea."

The nurse sets my hand down on the blanket. "You might have planned ahead better. But everything was closed."

"I passed a vending machine but thought stopping would be a waste of time."

"Staying healthy isn't ever a waste of time."

I wrinkle my nose at that. "So, am I okay now?"

"Yes. The doctors gave you a glucose injection. That's the IV in your arm."

I look down at my arm. "Oh. Lovely."

"How are you feeling?"

I shrug. "Less like puking."

The nurse smiles. "That's a good sign."

I remember Sunshine and sit up straight. "Did Sunshine come with? Or is she still at the airport?"

"Ms. Ballanger is here. She's in the waiting room."

"Can I see her? I have to see her."

The nurse nods. "I'll send for her."

She leaves and I lie back against the pillows. I notice that I'm in one of those god-awful hospital gowns. My boxers are on underneath, thank the Lord. I hope I don't look too gross.

I wonder where all my stuff is—my clothes, my guitar, my phone…I look around for them. My phone is on the little table next to the bed, my clothes are on the dresser type-thing next to it, and my guitar case is on the floor beside that. Good; all of my stuff is safe. I lie back against the pillows and close my eyes for a second as I wait for Sunshine to come.

Chapter Twenty-six

A nurse tells me that he's asking for me. I shed the blanket and get, up following the nurse through the doors that I watch an unconscious Abbot Jennings go through about an hour ago.

We enter the private room that he's in.

"It looks like he fell asleep," the nurse states.

"Is that okay?"

"That's fine. It's four in the morning, after all. Would you like to stay with him?"

"Yes, please."

"All right. I'll leave you two alone." She smiles and leaves, closing the door behind her.

I sigh and look across the room at Mouse. He is lying in a bed with the top half slightly elevated. Slowly, I walk towards him. His skin is pasty, and clammy-looking, and his hair looks like it could use a wash. He is wearing a hospital gown with tiny polar bears all over it.

I find a chair and pull it up to the bed. I sit in it and watch Mouse as he sleeps. My eyes fall to his arm, and the wires and tubes attached to it. I've gotten sort of used to them by now, and instead of being scared of them, I'm thankful that they are keeping him alive.

I concentrate on the constant beeping of the monitor watching over his heart. The heart that loves me. I glance out the window for a second and see that snow is gently falling down everywhere. Thinking about snow takes me back to our first (and only) Christmas together.

We exchanged presents on December 23rd, since we would both be busy with our families the next day and on Christmas. While his dad was at work, and his mom had taken his sisters with her to do a little last minute Christmas shopping, we sat by his Christmas tree with presents for each other behind our backs, Christmas songs playing on the radio, and sugar cookies in the oven. We both had streaks of flour on our ugly sweaters from where we'd flung handfuls of the stuff at each other.

"You first," he said.

"No, you first." We'd been tossing this back and forth for a few minutes by now.

"I want my present, Sunshine."

"Well, I want mine."

"You can have it after I get mine."

"Way to get into the holiday spirit, boyfriend."

"Thank you, hypocritical girlfriend."

I stuck my tongue out at him. He stuck his out right back.

"Why don't we open at the same time?" I suggested.

"I can't open your present and watch you open my present at the same time, Sunshine. Who do I look like to you…."

I stared at him and raised my eyebrow. "Are you going to finish that sentence?"

"I would, but I can't think of any people in pop culture known for their fantastic multitasking abilities."

"Neither can I. Let me have my present."

"Let *me* have mine."

I darted forward to grab it from behind him, but Mouse shot forward too, and kissed me, pushing the present further behind him. I pulled away from him.

"Ugh, you suck," I said, wiping his kiss off my mouth.

"You love me." He grinned smugly.

"But you suck."

"I'm sorry about that."

"No you're not."

"You're right."

"You'd suck less if you would just let me have my present."

"Nice try," he said. "Okay. Roshambeau for who goes first."

"Best two out of three?"

"Fine. Winner gets their present first."

"Okay," I held out my first, and he put out his. "Rock, paper, scissors."

We both put out rock. We went again. Mouse was scissors, I was rock. I smashed his scissors. We went again, and both put out paper. Again, and Mouse was paper, and I was rock. He covered me.

"You're going down, Ballanger," Mouse said with clenched teeth.

"Don't be so sure. Rock, paper, scissors!"

I was scissors and Mouse was paper. "Ha-ha!" I snipped his paper hand. "I win."

"Ugh. Fine." He crawled after the present

he had tossed away from himself. He sat back down with it and handed it over. "Merry Christmas, you smug son of a bitch."

"Thanks, sore loser." I carefully peeled off the red and white plaid wrapping paper. When I opened the box I discovered a pair of earrings inside.

"Ooh," I said, lifting one out with my fingertips and examining it. Two tiny, polished stones, one purple, the other blue, hung from copper earring hooks. "I like these."

"You do?"

"Yeah." I took out the earrings I was wearing and put in the new ones. "Where did you get them?"

"I made them. In Jewelry class."

I dropped my hands into my lap. "You made me earrings?"

Mouse nodded. "It wasn't that hard. Do you really like them? Because I got a B minus on the assignment."

"Mrs. Stroud would be lucky to have her boyfriend give her these earrings. I love them. Thanks."

"You're welcome. Merry Christmas, Sunshine." He kissed my cheek.

"Do you want your present now?" I asked him.

"So much."

"Okay." I took Mouse's present out from behind my back and handed it to him.

Mouse unwrapped the dark red headphones I got him. "Hey, you remembered that Laney broke my headphones." He opened them. "These are so fucking rad." He snapped them over his ears.

"They look good on you," I said.

"What?" he said loudly.

"They look good on you!" I shouted so he

could hear me.

He took them off and they hung around his neck. "Thanks. I love them a lot."

"I love *you* a lot."

"I love you, too."

As it got dark, we slow danced to classic Christmas tunes under mistletoe in pajama pants, ugly sweaters, handmade earrings, and new headphones. The only light was from the Christmas tree, and everything was sort of perfect.

I stop staring at the window when I see Mouse move out of the corner of my eye. I lean closer to his bed.

"Mouse?"

He takes a long, drowsy breath and opens his eyes slowly.

"Hey, Sunshine," he says in a scratchy, drowsy voice.

"Hi, Sleepyhead."

"Oh, I fell asleep? I was just going to close my eyes for a second until you came in."

"Hey, it's okay, Mouse. You're allowed to sleep in a hospital. How are you?"

"I'm alright." He smiles slowly at me. "I'm glad you came."

I look down at me lap. "I wasn't going to leave you alone in a hospital in Denver."

"Thanks." Mouse sits up and yawns. "So…God, what time is it?"

I look at the clock on the wall. "Four thirty in the morning."

"My sleep schedule is going to be so fucked up after this."

"I know, right?"

Mouse plays with his hospital bracelet. "So, um…I…about earlier. In the bathroom?"

I clear my throat and pull all my hair over onto one shoulder. I wipe my clammy hands on my jeans. "Yeah. I was going to talk to you about that, actually."

"What were you saying before—?"

"You don't love me, Mouse," I interrupt.

He blinks at me. "What?"

"I mean, it's impossible. Ten hours isn't enough to make up for five years of lost time. You can't possibly know me well enough now to love me. You're just…you're bored. You've got cabin fever."

Mouse stares at me with wide eyes. I curl my hands into my sweater sleeves and stare down at them.

"Maybe you're just infatuated. Or you like the idea of me. But I'm not the same girl you loved five years ago, Mouse."

"I know that," he says. "But that doesn't change the way I feel about you."

I bend back the fingers on my left hand with the fingers of my right. "You don't feel anything. You can't love me. You don't know me anymore."

"But I do. I know that you're determined and smart and ambitious. And forgiving and funny. You're stronger now. You're everything you used to be, and you're better. You're older."

I look up at him again. "Mouse, no. One night in an airport isn't nearly enough time to know all of that."

"Yes, it is."

"Mouse, you don't love me."

"I do love you, Sunshine," he insists.

"Mouse, you…you can't."

"I don't understand. What do you mean, I can't?"

"You think that you love me, but you don't. You think you love me because you need to. You need something to keep you sane while you're stuck here in Denver. And maybe being with me brings up old emotions, but that's all they are. A good love isn't made of a washed-up past."

"Sunshine, you're not making any sense. You said earlier—"

"Screw what I said earlier, Mouse. It wasn't real. I was just overtired, just like you're overtired."

Mouse furrows his brow. "Sunshine, please don't try to brush away my feelings like that. It's insulting."

"But it's the truth."

"No, it's not. I love you."

"No. You can't," I whisper. "You don't."

Mouse lets out a breathy laugh. "Okay, you can't do this. I'm not going to let you do this."

"Let me do what?"

"You don't get to tell me how I feel. You don't get to choose who I love. You may not want it to be true, and I understand that. But that doesn't mean it isn't true. You don't get to tell me when I get to... feel things. For people. That belongs to me, Sunshine. Not you."

I clench my fists until I feel my fingernails cut into my palms. Which is quite the feat, seeing as how my fingernails are bitten down pretty well.

"Mouse, please..."

"I love you."

"No, I need you to..."

"I *love you*."

"Mouse, you don't." My eyes sting with tears.

"I love you, Sunshine," he says loudly and firmly. "I've loved you forever. I love you now. And I'll love you tomorrow. Nothing you say, no matter times you interrupt me, that isn't going to change. And I'm sorry if that's not what you wanna hear, but it's true. Do you understand?""

"No." Because I don't. I feel the same way, and I still don't understand.

Mouse sighs and scrubs his hand sin his hair. "Well, can you at least deal with it?"

I sniff and sigh. "No. Not really."

There's a short bout of silence.

"Can I ask you why?"

"No." A tear falls down my cheek and I lower my head.

"I'm…going to anyway. Why can't you deal with it? Not that you should have to, I guess. I'm just kind of curious."

I drop my face into my hands. I take a shaky, sobby breath.

"I can't deal with you loving me because it fills me with all this false hope. It makes me want to find a way for this to work. It makes me want to fly down for your birthday to see you. It makes me want to Skype you before I go to sleep at night. It makes me want to do whatever it takes to be with you."

I lift my head and look at him for a moment. Meeting his gaze right now is too much, so instead I stare at his legs.

"Because I love you, too. And it makes no sense. And it's so fucking inconvenient, and I tried my very hardest to not love you, but then you played 'Moon River', and then you played that goddamn Mountain Goats song I mentioned to you one time a million years ago. And then my heart stopped listening to my mind, and I couldn't control anything anymore. And loving you, I can't deal with it. Because there's nothing that can happen after we both board our planes and fly off in different directions."

I dare to look at him again, and it shatters me. He looks stunned. His eyes are full of tears that drop down his cheeks and the bridge of his nose. His mouth is partially open. His eyebrows pinch together for a soft second. It sends me over the edge of a cliff I've been falling from and climbing back to the top of all day long.

"Soleil," he breathes. "Oh my God."

"I know." I laugh, smearing my tears around on my face. "It sucks."

He moves over on his bed. "Get up here."

I shake my head, even though I want to do nothing else as much as that.

"Please. I need to touch you. I might still be sleeping." His voice is slow and dazed.

"You aren't. And touching me wouldn't prove anything, anyway."

"It would prove that you're real." There are more tears. His voice shakes. "That this is real, and I'm awake, and you love me."

"I shouldn't love you," I whisper as more tears tumble down my cheeks.

"But you do," Mouse replies, his voice

cracking. "You love me, and I need you here, closer to me, so I can hold your hand and know that this isn't some sick dream."

"Isn't seeing me enough?"

"Seeing you was never enough."

I wring my hands. "Will it ever be?"

Mouse sighs and tips his head back, looking at the fluorescent lights on the ceiling. He swallows, and brings his head back down. His voice is stronger and the most sure it's ever been. "I don't care about 'ever'. I only care about now."

I give a choking sob.

Mouse takes a deep breath and rubs his eyes. He lets out a long breath then drops his hands into his lap. "Can we forget about what happens later and just be thankful for now? And this?" Mouse asks.

Just for now. Just for this. "We can try," I offer.

"Thank you."

I sniff. "You're welcome."

"Will you come up here now?"

I get out of my seat and climb onto the bed. I lie on my side, propping my head up in my hand.

Mouse holds his hand up, his fingers spread apart. My own fingers fill the negative space. Mouse brings our hands to his lips, and kisses the back of mine.

"Good morning, Sunshine."

I take a deep breath, and let it out. A wobbling smile spreads across my face. "Good morning, Mouse."

"I love you."

"I love you, too."

Mouse smiles. It isn't the blue ribbon grin. It's weary and lost and passionate and happy. The same exact smile on his face from when I fell in love with him. And I sit up and kiss the smile right from his face.

I guess Mouse wasn't expecting me to do that, since he opens his mouth and gasps. Then he kisses me back. His hands come up to my face, and I feel his thumbs brush away the tears stained onto my cheeks. My hands rest on his neck. I open my mouth and accept his tongue into it. We're past the point of chaste kisses.

Mouse's hand moves to the back of my neck, and he draws me down to lie against him. I put my hands on his shoulders, and push deeper into him, consuming and exploring all of his new cells.

We don't pull back until our lips are numb. And even then, it's just for a second. I push his hair out of his face, and he tucks my hair behind my ear, then grazes his hand down to my lips, where his thumb brushes softly over them. His smile is full of awe. He's in awe of *me*. I let my forehead fall to rest against his.

"I like this Now," I say softly.

"So do I." His hand goes up and down my back.

"Are you okay?" I ask.

"I'm amazing."

"You're sure? I'm not pulling on any of your IVs or anything?"

"Only thing you're pulling is my heartstrings."

I groan, resting my head on his shoulder and kissing it. "You're the king of Mushtopia."

"I will wear my crown with pride." He guides our faces back together and he kisses me again.

(Mouse)

This is real. She is real. We are real. I've never liked hospitals so much.

Or hated them. Because there's not an ounce of privacy.

The moment my fingers go beneath the hem of Sunshine's top, I hear the door open. We jump apart from each other. A female doctor steps into the room. Her eyes widen at our current state of being.

"Um. Hi there. Sorry for…interrupting. I'm just here to see if you're clear to get checked out of the hospital."

"Oh. Sure. Thanks."

Sunshine gets off of the hospital bed and stands out of the doctor's way. She puts her hand in mine. The doctor reads the clipboard at the end of my bed.

"How are you feeling now, Abbot?" she asks.

"Um. A lot better, thanks."

She lowers the clipboard and smiles. "It looks like you're all set. Let me just get a nurse in here to unhook you from these IVs, and then if you want to get dressed and get your stuff together, you can get checked out."

"Thanks," I say.

"You're welcome. Hope your day gets better." She leaves.

Sunshine and I are left alone again.

"Do you want to get a room at one of the airport hotels?" Sunshine asks. "I don't want to sleep on another airport couch as long as I live."

"Yes. *Yes*. Hand me my phone, I'll call one of them."

"Let me. You still have to get unhooked from all of these wires and junk."

I smile at her, and she leans down and kisses me.

A nurse, the same one from earlier, comes into the room. Sunshine steps away again, smiling bashfully and pushing her hair back. She takes out her phone and starts tapping away on it. The nurse extracts the tubes and needles from my arm and hand. She covers the punctures with a few bandages.

"There, you're all set. Doctor Humphrey has your papers for release at the front desk."

"Thanks." I sit up.

"No problem. Have a good day. Or night. Whatever it is outside. I haven't really had a chance to check."

"Thanks. You too."

The nurse leaves, and we're actually alone now.

"Well that was fun," I say.

"What was fun?"

"This entire day has been fun. The being admitted to the hospital was definitely a high point for me, though, gotta be honest."

Sunshine stares at me with wavering patience. "So do you want me to leave while you get dressed?"

I shrug. "It doesn't matter." I toss back the covers and get my clothes from the table. "I think I'll change in the bathroom. I'm dying for a shower. If that's okay."

"Sure. You definitely need it. You're hair's kind of gross right now."

"Please Sunshine, tell me how you really feel about my current state of hygiene." I untie my hospital gown and toss it on the bed.

Sunshine looks me up and down in a way that is the opposite of subtle. She meets my eyes again, and says, "You could also do with a shave." She dials a number on her phone and holds it to her ear, turning her back to me.

I stick my tongue out and go into the bathroom.

Twenty minutes later, we're in a taxi on the way to a hotel near the airport. There is one seat between Sunshine and I, and our hands there, one on top of the other. Mine on top of hers. We don't talk the entire way there.

Sunshine checks us in, and we take the elevator up to the fourth floor, and she slides her key into the slot on the door and pushes it open. We find our luggage already waiting for us.

After taking off our shoes, we both collapse onto the same bed. I'm out as soon as I close my eyes.

Chapter Twenty-seven

I wake up but don't open my eyes. My neck aches and my teeth are in desperate need of brushing. My hair is a frizzy mess, I'm sure of it. And sleeping in jeans is not, nor will it ever be, comfortable.

But when I open my eyes, I know that Mouse will be there. I know his face will be only inches from my face, and his hands will be covered by his sweater sleeves. I know his legs will be linked loosely with mine. I know all of these because I can feel them. And knowing all of these things completely diminishes the unpleasantness of fuzzy teeth, frizzy hair, and sore necks.

So I don't open my eyes until my neck pain shoots through to my skull, and running my tongue along my teeth literally makes me shudder with disgust. One eye, and then the other.

Mouse is just as I knew he would be. And his eyes are open, too. They smile at me, and he winds his sweatered hands around my middle, drawing me closer. He hides his face in my frizzy hair.

"What time is it?" he asks.

I look over his shoulder at the clock on the nightstand. "Seven AM."

"Errrmmm," he mumbles and rubs my back. "How was your sleep?"

"Good. Kind of. I want to brush my teeth. And take off my pants. And take pain reliever."

"Well, you should…" Mouse yawns, and I feel his warm breath on my neck. "…go do those things."

"I think I will." I get out of the bed, and get my toothbrush, a bottle of painkillers, and a pair of boxers out of my suitcase. I go into the bathroom, brush my teeth, change, and toss back two Tylenol.

I go back to the main room and find Mouse holding his phone over his head, his thumb scrolling across the screen.

"Hi," he says, looking past his arms at me.

"Hey." I lie on my stomach, my hands twisting together in my shirt sleeves.

"Feel better?"

"Much, thank you."

Mouse put his phone down. "Now what do we do?"

I take a long breath through my nose and sigh. "Well, I think there are two main options. We could talk about what's going to happen with whatever…" I make a back and forth gesture at us with my hands. "…whatever it is that we're doing. Or, we could ignore that responsibility and make out again."

"I like that idea," Mouse states.

"So do I."

"But we've already done that. And we have yet to talk. So…we should probably maybe do that."

"Probably." I pout.

He kisses my dramatically protruding bottom lip.

I laugh and sit up.

"Okay, let's list off the possible options we have for going forward in this… whatever it is, and the pros and cons each of them hold." Mouse pushes himself into an upright position and crosses his legs.

"Ooh, okay. I did this earlier with June."

"Who is June?"

"Juniper. My best friend."

"Oh, you have friends in Chicago?"

"Yes, I have friends in Chicago," I say in a mocking voice.

"Well, obviously you would. You're cool and stuff. So what's this Juniper like?"

"Her hair is blue. And…She's…cool and stuff." Cooler than me. Too cool to put into words.

"So, you wanna be a writer?" He smirks.

I shove his arm. "Oh, shut up."

"Ow," he yanks his arm away. "Careful. IV. Still sore."

"Ahh," I wince, and lightly kiss the part of his arm I shoved. "Sorry."

He flashes a little smile at me as a sign of forgiveness. "Anyway, this list. Option number one?"

"We agree that nothing should happen after we get on our planes, but exchange email addresses and phone numbers so we can keep in touch."

"Not bad. Pros?"

"We get to be somewhat involved in each other's lives while not having to big an influence on each other."

"True. Cons?"

"We probably won't see each other, and we won't be anything but pen pals."

"Does seem like a downgrade."

"I agree. So, what is option two?"

"We...part ways amicably at the airport, but nothing happens beyond that. No numbers, no email. No Twitter. Just rip it off like an old Band-Aid."

"Yum. Pros?"

Mouse frowns. "None, besides...nah. I've got nothing."

"Okay. Cons?"

"Literally every part of that plan."

I sigh. "Yeah. It's kind of...painful."

"I agree. So, shall we consider option three?"

"Option three, we decide to try another

long-distance relationship. We exchange information on any and all social media platforms, get numbers, emails and Skype usernames, and figure out a reasonable amount of times to visit each other each month."

"What are the pros of option three?"

I stare down at my hands. "We'll be actually dating. We can work towards an endpoint where we actually live in the same place, or at least city. It gives us time to grow, and also allows us to support each other while we work to discover who we are and get where we want to be."

"Hmm. Compelling points. Cons?"

"Well…we tried the distance thing once, and it failed, so who's to say it won't again? What if it turns toxic, what if we feel smothered or…trapped, or something. Should we just move on? Are we too different now?"

"I don't know. Do you think we are?"

I shrug. "I know that we've changed. Or at

least grown."

"Is that bad?"

"Not all bad."

"Saying 'not all bad' makes it sound like there is some bad," Mouse remarks.

"You're right. It does."

"What's bad about how we've changed?"

I flip over onto my back. "I don't know. It's not…bad, exactly. I mean it…it isn't good."

"Are you talking about my diabetes?"

"…Yes."

Mouse nods. "Right."

"I'm sorry," I say softly, staring down at the comforter on the bed.

"No, you don't have to be sorry. I don't particularly like it, either. But that's not exactly something you would have to deal with if we were to commit to a long-distance relationship."

"Is that a pro?"

"You tell me, Sunshine."

I don't say anything.

Mouse changes the subject. "So, it seems like all of the cons are more like possible issues. Issues that could be addressed, or worked around. But I feel like since we have the freedom to see each other whenever we want to, you know, within reason, we wouldn't feel so inaccessible to each other. It would feel more like a relationship. It would be…more valid."

"Yeah. I guess so." My tone is guarded. I'm still embarrassed about what I said before.

Mouse sits up. "I think we've been responsible enough for a while. Would you like to make out now?"

I feel my shoulders relax, and smile and nod.

"Cool," Mouse says, and leans down over me, and catches my lips between his. I close my eyes and I put my hand on the back of his neck.

The bed is soft, and Mouse is equal parts gentle and demanding. I feel as if something changed in the way he kisses since we were dating. He was demanding then, too, but the way he is kissing me now feels desperate. Like every second we have must be spent with our lips put together. It's like kissing me is all he knows how to do.

His fingers play with the hem of my shirt. He starts pushing it up higher, and I know how this is going to end up.

I pull his cardigan off of him, and let it drop to the floor. Mouse's mouth moves to my neck. I twist my head so I can bury my nose in his hair. I breathe in. He smells like tobacco, but with some sort of sweet undertone.

"You still smoke?" I ask, tilting my head back as he kisses my throat.

"No," he says between kisses. "I have pipe tobacco that I keep in a satchel in my dresser drawer because I like the smell."

"Pipe tobacco? God, pretentious much?"

He kisses me again and sighs. "Shut up."

"I'm kidding. I like it."

"Thanks. I'm going to take off your shirt now."

"Go for it." I arch my back so he can roll the hem up over my torso. He does, and I lift my arms up so he can take it off the rest of the way. It goes on the floor with his cardigan.

Mouse leans back and away, combing his fingers through my hair, taming the flyaways. He gathers it all up in his hands and fans it out on the pillow.

He smiles fondly. "I love you, Sunshine."

"You do? I had no idea."

"Well, now you know." Mouse lay on his side, his thumb stroking my shoulder. "I love you, Sunshine. And I'm so happy that I found you again. No matter what happens later, I am so very glad to be with you now. There's no place I would rather be than here with you."

My heart swells. I roll over onto him, straddling his sides, and hauling him up so I can take off his shirt. I shove it off the bed, and hold his face in my hands. My fingers run across every new contour of his face. My fingers trace his jawline, and it's so wonderful that I bow my head to kiss it three times in a row.

Mouse lays down, pulling me down with him. Our stomachs are pressed together, and our breaths sync up. Each breath he breathes in is a breath I breathe out.

I put my head on my chest. My fingers brush the fated insulin pump, and it feels so foreign that my hands jump back like I touched a hot burner on a stove. I tentatively turn my fingertips over it again, and then trace my finger around it. Mouse's skin blossoms with reddish pink spots. He smiles at me.

"I love you, too, Mouse. I love the way

you make me feel so bright."

"You're Sunshine. You're bright all on your own."

"Sunshine is what I'm called, not what I am."

"You're sunshine to me," Mouse says, his fingers tracing shapes onto my back. "You're everything to me."

"Hm." I say softly. "I'll take that."

His hand runs along the side of my torso. "It's all I've got to give to you."

I kiss him again. Harder, longer, faster. This is all the time I have with him, and every moment of it needs to be spent like this. With him. My voice may not be able to relate to Mouse exactly how much I love him, but maybe my mouth can. Kissing him is all I know how to do.

(Mouse)

I didn't ever think we'd be together like this again. The morning that I left for Wisconsin, Sunshine snuck out of my room and left her earring behind, along with a French poem. I'd let myself believe it then, but after we broke up, of course I didn't believe it anymore.

I heard what she said before she got out of bed, too. That she would love me, for as long and for as far as either of us care to go.

That's the tiny little spark of hope that drove me to sing her that song. I was hoping what she'd said then was still true. I guess I was right.

And somehow we're both here, like this. And neither of us lie still until the Sun comes up.

Chapter Twenty-eight

When it's all over, we lie together, side by side and facing each other, tired and slow and happy.

"This is disturbingly similar to the last time we had sex, isn't it." Mouse says.

"Early morning…parting ways in a few hours, much to our chagrin. It's déjà vu all over again."

"I still remember what you said to me before you left for good that morning."

"What? I thought you were asleep during that."

"I wasn't. I was thinking about you. And then I heard you walking to the doorway, and you said… 'Abbot Wilson Jennings, I love you. I'll love you no matter where you go. I will love you as long as you smile the way that you smile, and as long as you say my name the wonderful way that you do. I'll love you for as long as your eyes shine and your shoulders relax when you see me. For as long, and for as far, as either of us care to go.'"

"You remember all of that?"

"It's all I could think about for most of the time I was with you last night."

I stare at his freckled shoulder, and say quietly, "Every time your said my name, it was like a punch to the gut."

Mouse raises his eyebrows.

I rephrase myself. "I mean, I was just overcome by it all.I was trying to hard not to love you, but you made it so easy to fall again. You're so much brighter, stronger. You're really starting to figure yourself out, and it shows."

"You're different, too. You know what you want, and nothing stops you. You're confident, you assert yourself more. You look out for yourself. I'm glad you're doing that."

I smile. "Thank you."

He smiles back. My eyes lower down to his shoulder freckles again. I want to play connect the dots with them. I roll over and open the nightstand drawer, finding a pad of paper and a pen inside. I uncap the pen with my teeth and face Mouse.

"What are you doing with that pen?" he asks.

I reach forward and touch the tip of the pen to his skin.

"Hey, now." He edges away.

"No no, you have to stay still, or it'll get ruined."

"You aren't drawing on me."

"What, are you afraid you're gonna get ink poisoning? Are you a white suburban mom?"

Mouse fidgets. "No…"

"I'm not gonna draw a dick on you or anything. Calm down, would you? Ink comes off."

"Well, what are you going to draw on me, if not dicks?"

I shrug. "I don't know yet. We'll see where the freckles take me."

Mouse sighs. "Only because I love you."

"Fair enough." I move closer to Mouse and lift my left hand again to draw a line from one freckle to the other. Until I get an idea of what I'm going to sketch, I use short lines that can be turned into anything. I lean on my other hand for support as I keep drawing.

Mouse closes his eyes and his body goes so relaxed that I know that he's going to fall asleep. I draw more gently, and make sure he doesn't roll over and smear the ink.

When I'm done and Mouse breathes deeply as he sleeps, I lean back and squint to make sure my connect-the-freckles fox actually looks like a fox. As if there was anything I could do about it if it didn't. But it looks pretty good to me, so I put the cap back on my pen and decide to check the flight schedule.

I boot my Mac up and tap my feet against the mattress while I wait for my desktop to open. Mouse is right, I probably should put a password on this thing.

I double-click on the Google Chrome icon and open my bookmark of the flight schedule. Some of the non-international flights have come back online, and I see that Portland is boarding at 3:30. I scroll down to Chicago. It's scheduled to take off at twelve PM. I check the time. It's nine, so that leaves me with three hours. Three hours left to be with Mouse. Three hours left to make a decision about this. About what will happen to us when we go back home. I sigh and close the laptop.

"Is something wrong, Sunshine?" Mouse has woken up. He rubs the sleep out of his eyes.

"Our flights are back online."

Mouse frowns. "When do they leave?"

"Chicago is at noon. Portland is three-thirty."

"Wow. So…we should come to a decision shouldn't we? All of our options. We have to actually pick one now."

I nod. "It looks that way."

Mouse looks down at the comforter.

"It was going to happen anyway, Mouse."

"I know," he says quietly.

"How about this: Let's take some time to think about it. We'll get dressed and do whatever else we need to do to get ready, then we'll talk. Okay?"

Mouse nods. "Alright."

Chapter Twenty-nine

I step out of the shower and swipe the fog from the mirror. My tired face stares at me. I get dressed in leggings and my favorite old sweater before I tie my hair up into a mess of a bun that flops off-kilter at the back of my head, with stray pieces falling in damp, kinky curls at my temples and the nape of my neck.

I stand for a minute with my hand on the doorknob, working up the courage to twist it open and face the person on the other side and the choices we have to make.

With a long sigh, I walk through the door to find Mouse by the window, staring out at the blinding white blanket of snow covering it all. He turns and the smile he gives to me doesn't reach his eyes by a long shot.

"Thanks for the fox," he says, shrugging the shoulder I had drawn on.

"You're welcome." I sit down on the bed. "Are you ready?"

"As I'll ever be," he says, shoving his hands in his pockets and sitting on the edge, beside me.

I pick at one of my hangnails instead of meeting his gaze. A long stretch of quiet, the result of hours of tension, hangs in the air.

"I think we should try again," I say at the same time Mouse says,

"I don't think we should see each other."

My head snaps up. Mouse blinks at me. "What?"

"I...I mean, it wouldn't be impossible. You said so yourself." I reply.

"Well, yes, but... I didn't think you'd want that. I thought you'd want to focus on your writing. I didn't think you wanted to be pining all of the time."

"I wouldn't be. Not with the promise of seeing you regularly."

"Really?"

"What do *you* want, Mouse?"

"I want you to be happy."

"I want *you* to be happy."

"That doesn't get us anywhere," Mouse says, frustrated, as he leans back in his seat.

"Which option do you like more?"

"Do you mean would I rather date the person I am in love with or would I rather never see or contact her again? Take a guess, Sunshine."

"I would, but you completely contradicted what I thought you were going to say when you said you didn't think we should see each other."

"Is that what you want, Sunshine? Do you want us to date again?"

I stammer a moment, unsure of what I want until real words come from my mouth. "I want us to be in the same place, with lives and careers that we're happy with."

"I'd like that, too, but that's not us now.

That's us in…I don't know. It seems like you're closer to that goal than I am. Are you saying you want to wait?"

"No, that's almost the exact same thing as a long-distance relationship. Except it's worse, because there's none of the contact and all of the excruciating time, with no foreseeable endpoint."

"So you want to date now?"

"I want happiness," I repeat.

"Sunshine." Mouse looks away from me and sighs. He looks back and shrugs his shoulders, as if the answer is simple, and obvious. "All I need to be happy is you. I can make a life anywhere."

"I don't want your life to depend on where I live, Mouse."

"Sunshine." Mouse leans forward again, grabbing my hands and rubbing his thumbs on the back of them. "I need you to understand something: I would much, much rather live with you in your world than live without you in my world."

The skin between my brows pinches together and I give a tearful sigh.

He sits closer to me. He reaches up and strokes my cheek, brushing away phantom tears. "There are bookstores in Chicago, Sunshine. And a pretty decent music scene. I could be moved out of my house within a few weeks."

"Wait, are you talking about moving?"

His hand moves to my hair, twisting a tendril of it gently between his fingers. He looks at it instead of me. "Yes, if that's what sounds like the best option."

"You…can't do that. What if we break up? You aren't moving across the country from some girl you met ten hours ago. I won't let you do that."

Our eyes meet again. He widens his eyes. "I'm not moving for 'some girl'. I would be moving for you. Sunshine."

"I don't care."

Mouse sighs and folds his arms. "Okay…so are we doing long-distance, then?"

I groan, fall against the pillows and cover my face. "I don't *know*."

"I need you to know, Sunshine. We don't have time for uncertainty."

I lift my head, and bite at him, "I know that, okay? Do you really think I don't know that? Because I do. I know, I know that in two and a half hours, I will be gone from you again. I know that there's no time, and that just makes it harder to make a choice."

Mouse frowns. "I know. I'm sorry. I just…agh." He tips his head back. "Lord Almighty."

I scoff at the situation we have put ourselves in. We just *had* to go and fall in love.

Mouse gets up from the bed.

"Where are you going?" I ask, sitting up

again.

"Nowhere, Sunshine." His voice is tense as he walks to the counter.

"Well, what are you doing?"

"I'm making tea."

"Oh. Can you make me some?"

"I was already planning to."

"Thank you."

Mouse doesn't reply. I sit silently for a minute or two, then get up from bed and walk behind him, putting my arms around his middle like a seatbelt.

"I love you, Mouse. I just don't want you to feel like you have to move for me. I don't think I want you to do that. Not now, when you haven't got your life figured out yet."

Mouse sets two mugs on the counter. "Maybe my life isn't in Portland. Maybe it's with you. In Chicago. Maybe this is all part of some greater plan."

"I thought you didn't believe in that kind of stuff."

Mouse shrugged. "I don't know what I believe very much right now."

"Oh, Mouse." I press my forehead against his spine.

I feel the tension in his body fall away. He turns around and hugs me.

"I'm sorry if I'm being an asshole. I won't move if that's not what you want. I'll keep looking for what I want to do in Portland. Or at least figuring out a good reason to live in Chicago. Besides the fact that you live there, too."

"Thank you, Mouse. That's all I ask. I want more for you than just the promise of me."

"And I want you to understand that all I need is the promise of you. Of us."

I move back to look at his eyes. "I'm not all you need. Not financially. Not entirely emotionally. Not physically. There is more to life than love."

"You don't think love is the most important?"

I'm not sure that it is. Not anymore. "I…never said that. But love doesn't keep you healthy. Love doesn't keep a roof over your head."

"You're more different than I thought," Mouse says. The microwave goes off. He takes the hot water out and pours water into the two waiting mugs.

"What does that mean?"

"Well, 17 year-old Sunshine put so much faith in love. You were so sure that we loved each other enough to wait until college to be together. So sure that if we loved each other, everything else would follow. Why don't you believe that anymore?"

"Because it didn't turn out to be true. Our love wasn't enough. We still broke up. It's not that I don't believe in love anymore, it's just that I can't bet on it. I can't count on love to keep me safe."

"Are you sure that you love me? Because I feel like if you did, you would be able to trust me more." Mouse hands me the steaming mug of tea.

I take it, lowering my head over it and letting the steam warm my face. I bob the tea bag up and down. "I do trust you, Mouse. And I do love you. I just can't trust my instincts when it comes to love these days."

"Is that because of me? Or the other guy you mentioned earlier?"

"I don't know which answer you want." I say, sitting at the small table by the window.

Mouse picks up his own mug of tea and sits down across from me. "I want whichever answer is the truth."

"Because of you. And because of the other guy…Andrew."

"Andrew?" Mouse frowns "What did Andrew do?"

"He cheated on me. Six months ago, yesterday. I almost moved to New Zealand after college with him. For him. But then I caught him making out with some other girl in *my* apartment."

I see a flicker of the younger Mouse in his eyes. "What a piece of shit."

"That's what I said. After I punched him in the face."

He raises his brows. "Wow. Go, Sunshine."

"I'd just gotten out of self-defense class and had a lot of adrenaline going through me still."

"He totally deserved it."

I grip the handle of my mug. "He really did," I grumble into it.

Mouse takes a sip of tea then puts his mug

down. "Okay: So you love me. And you trust me. But you don't trust love. Because of me."

"Partially because of you."

"And yet you still love me."

"Yes."

"That doesn't make sense. How can you love someone and not believe in, or trust in love?

"You and Andrew changed the way I feel about love in different ways. Because of you, I lost my faith in the idea that love can wait. Because of Andrew, I stopped believing that love meant completely changing your life for one person."

Mouse scratches his head. "I don't think love necessarily means you have to change your life. But love isn't love if you aren't willing to try to make it work. And sometimes trying involves things like moving, or waiting. And that's something that I didn't know when I was sixteen. If I did, I wouldn't have so cracked so easily when my dad kept badgering me about you."

I massage my temples.

"I think love is making mistakes, and learning from them and not worrying that the other person will leave if you screw up every now and then," Mouse says. "Love is messy and hard and scary and wild. Love is not knowing what the hell you're doing, but knowing that you don't have to figure it out alone. Love isn't limited by miles, only by how much you believe in it."

I glance up wearily at him.

"I would be honored to be the person who makes you believe in love again, Sunshine. I mean, I think we both know you believe in it a little. Enough to love me. Or enough to want to love me."

"I do believe in love," I insist. "But I also believe that love isn't a choice. It just happens, whether we want it to or not. And I do love you, Mouse. I keep telling you that. I don't *want* to love you, but I *do* love you. I don't want to because it's too hard right now. I want to believe we can find some way for this to work, some happy medium, but it's been so long since I've been loved well that being absolutely sure that love conquers all, or whatever, is a luxury that I don't have anymore."

His eyes. Like being felt. I hate that I love that he does this. He knows that he shouldn't touch me right now, so he's finding a different way to get through to me. "I'm really sorry to hear that, Sunshine. But how are you ever going to trust anything without taking a chance?"

I don't have an argument for that. We sit quietly until our cups of tea are empty. It is half past ten now. I should leave for the airport soon. I should tell him I need to get ready.

"Mouse?" I say.

"Yeah?"

I decide not to tell him. "Does anyone call you Mouse in Portland?"

"No. Nobody does. I'm Abbot there. I'm Abbot to basically everyone that's not my parents, sisters, or you."

"Do you still like being called Mouse?"

"It depends. I like being called Mouse by my sisters. And by you. But I'm so fed up with my dad these days that I feel like we don't have the sort of relationship where nicknames are appropriate."

"I'm sorry. About how shitty stuff with him is for you."

"Don't worry about me. I don't have to see him that much. I'm worried about my mom and my sisters."

"...."

"..."

"Hey, Mouse?"

"Yeah?"

"Is it okay if I take a little more time to think about it? Just until before I have to get on my plane. Like, a good amount of time before. So we can swap phone numbers or whatever we have to do."

"Sure. Absolutely. Whatever you want."

"Thank you. Thank you so much for understanding. I love you."

He smiles, but it looks like it hurts him to. "I love you, too."

(Mouse)

Sunshine just asked me for more time to make a decision about us. I said yes, of course, but it's making me so anxious. All her negative talk about not trusting love anymore really makes me believe that she doesn't think we're worth fighting for. Part of me isn't sure any of this matters. The other part is on his knees, trying to sweep up any scraps of hope he can find into his arms.

We spend the next half hour packing up, and everything feels so wrong. I want to slam down my clothes and take Sunshine by her shoulders and speak some sense into her.

I'd like to, but I can't, because nothing makes any sense. I want to believe that us being together makes sense, but I know that it doesn't. Not in her books. (*Sunshine and her books.*) And maybe not at all. Besides, Sunshine has always been a little stubborn.

It hurts. This silence; this not knowing. It creates an ache in my bones, heightened with every move I make. Looking at her makes it worse. Because she refuses to meet my eyes. Her back is to me at every possible chance.

I believe her when she says she loves me. But if I said it didn't hurt, knowing she didn't want to love me, I would be lying..

I zip up my suitcase from where it sits on the bed. Then, somewhat involuntarily, I am on my knees, my arms folded on the edge of my bed with my head resting on top of them. I breathe deeply and sigh the breath back out, because it's the only thing that will keep me from crying.

I feel Sunshine's hand alight on my shoulder. "Mouse?" she says.

I push my hands through my hair and dig my fingers into the back of my neck.

"Are you okay?" She must have just knelt down beside me, because I can feel her leg brush against mine.

I shake my head. "No."

Chapter Thirty

Mouse isn't okay. I just asked him. And it's because of me. I don't have to ask to know it's about me. It's about how all of my romantic conquests have failed, and as a result, my faith in love is fading.

But my faith in love and my faith in Mouse are not mutually exclusive. I don't think I've made that clear enough.

"Mouse," I rubbed his back and kissed his shoulder. "I do love you. I believe that love is real. I believe in you. I believe that you want this to work. And I know that the way I talk about loving you doesn't make it sound this way, but I want this to work, too. I'm just not sure how healthy it will be for us. I don't know if knowing that you love me will be enough to keep me from going insane. I want to be with you, Mouse. So much. But I also want what's best for the both of us. I just…I'm not sure that a relationship is in the cards for us right now."

"What if being with you is what's best for me?" he says in a rough whisper from where he kneels at the foot of the bed.

"How can you know that right now? Don't you think it would take a few months of long-distance before we could tell how serious we are about this?"

"How much more serious can I be than being in love with you? What else do you *want*?"

I could repeat myself, or I could say what I really want. I squeeze my eyes closed and let out the truth. "I want you to be okay with the idea of waiting. I want you to be rational with this. If I'm going to start trusting love more, I need you to prove to me that this love is worth trusting. I need you to want my happiness. Like I know you do. I need you to just…be slow for me. I need you to stay where you are."

Mouse lifts his head. His eyes are pink. "Is that a decision I hear you making?"

I bite my lip, then drop my shoulders and

let it go. "I want a relationship with you, Mouse. I love you, and I want this to work. I want to try long-distance, with frequent trips to see each other, and plenty of Skype calls. This isn't going to be easy, and we're going to do a lot of meeting in the middle, but… I want this. I want you. But I want you to have a reason to come to Chicago besides me. Or at least, I want you to be doing something you love in Chicago. If you move there, you've gotta find a job you love to do. You can't just be there for me. You can be there because of me, but not just because of me. And if there is no foreseeable endpoint, nothing to work towards… if you don't know what you want to do after a year and a half, then we have to end it."

Mouse sighs and presses the heels of his hands into his eyes. "Thank you," he says. "I can do that. I will. I can be slow. We'll go so slow, Sunshine."

I smile at him, and take his face in my hands. His fingers loop around my wrists. "We're gonna be okay, Mouse."

"Yeah?"

"Yeah." I press my mouth to his. And he kisses me so slow.

(Mouse)

We're in another cab, this time to the airport. I sit in the middle, and Sunshine has the window seat behind the passenger seat. I'm holding Sunshine's hand, and it's clammy. Or maybe it's mine. We're both looking out the window on her side. Only I'm not so much looking through the window as I am looking at Sunshine's reflection in the window.

She bites her lip and glances down at the car lock. Her fingers twitch in my hand. I squeeze them and touch my mouth to her shoulder without really kissing it.

How cruel the world is—only a few hours with the girl I love before we get torn apart again. It could be worse, I know. I get to see her again, probably in a few months. And until then, I will remain a part of her life. I'm grateful I get to be in her life at all. But that doesn't mean saying goodbye is going to be easy now. In my experience, goodbye is never easy.

We arrive at the airport, and take our

luggage out of the trunk of the cab. In one hand, we both haul our suit cases behind us, and the pinkies on our other hands are linked together. We check in with our boarding passes, and then drop off our stuff, and walk through the airport and sit just outside the gate where Sunshine's flight boards.

Every part of me won't stop moving. My right leg bounces up and down, and my hand on my knee cap with it, my left hand strums my left leg like it's a guitar, I can't look at one place for too long, and I'm biting my lip.

Sunshine's toes are pointed in towards each other, and she slouches over her phone, her hair rendering her face impossible to see.

I stop bouncing around and check my watch. There's half an hour before she has to board.

Hey," I say, putting a hand on her back. She whips her head up and looks at me. "Want to get some breakfast before you go?"

Sunshine bites down on her lip, looks away from me a second, then looks back and nods. I put half a smile on my face and take her hand.

"Let's go, then."

Chapter Thirty-one

Mouse sits across from me at a table close to theexit of Woody Creek Bakery with a plate of quiche and fruit in front of him. I stare into my bowl of oatmeal, poking around the blueberries and walnuts.

I've just committed to dating Mouse again. And while I want to, I really, really do, I'm just not sure if it's right. I don't know if I can be strong enough to be in love with someone so far away. After it not working once. After Andrew. It's like getting a scab peeled from my heart and the wound being exposed, stinging and pink, threatening to bleed.

I lift my head and watch Mouse scribble on a napkin with a blue ink pen. "So, I'm giving you my phone number, Twitter handle, Skype username…which is the same as it was five years ago. Also, my email, and Tum…"

"Mouse," I blurt.

He looks up. "Yeah?"

My mouth is open, and the words I have to say claw their way up my throat. I say it in French, because it somehow feels easier. "I can't do this."

"Wh…" Mouse licks his lips. He replies in French, "What do you mean?"

"I…" I squeeze my eyes closed and shake my head. "I can't date you. I never should have said that I could."

I open my eyes back up. Mouse pales and stares down at the table. "Oh."

"I'm so sorry," I say, going back to English, my voice breaking. "I love you, Mouse, I honestly do…but we can't."

"Yeah." Mouse puts down the pen and wipes his hands on his jeans. "Yeah, no…I know. I get it."

I catch a flash of the painful twist in his features before he bows his head. He lifts it and forces himself to look at me. There's so much in his eyes. Pain and shock and sadness. All of it my fault. He pushes his chair out.

"I think I should go, then."

"No, no. We've still got twenty minutes. You don't have to go. Mouse and Sunshine 'til the break of dawn, remember?"

"The break of dawn has come and gone. It's daytime, Sunshine. And...and being with you now is...killing me. I need to go."

Mouse gets up so quickly that the table shakes, making his orange juice splash onto the table top. He turns and walks away without looking at me.

Just before he leaves the bakery, he turns around to face me.

"*Je t'aime*," he says. "*Je n'ai jamais arrêté de t'aimer. Je ne cesserai jamais de vous aimer. Je ne serai jamais désolée. Adieu, Soleil.*"

I start to say goodbye back, but he's already gone.

I mop up the spilled orange juice with the

napkin Mouse was writing on, before I get any ideas about calling him or something stupid like that.

(Mouse)

So this is a rough outline of how my life goes:

1. There's a big change in my life. I find it hard to adjust.

2. By utter chance, something good happens to me.

3. Things start turning up. I get comfortable in my new life.

4. This new life gets pulled out from under me, and I'm left sitting on my ass, with all of my pieces scattered on the floor.

5. I get scared and end up doing something stupid and self-destructive in my personal, psychotic attempt of coping.

Three guesses which stage I'm at now.

I've just walked out of the bakery where Sunshine and I were eating breakfast, and now I have no idea what to do. I end up walking into the first restroom I see. I lock myself in a stall and cover my face with my hands. I lean against a wall and take in as much breath as my lungs can hold.

I am most certain that this has been the worst Christmas vacation ever. I don't know why I was stupid enough to let myself get cozy with the idea that Sunshine would actually go through with another long-distance relationship. I should have seen this coming.

It wasn't even like she was wrong, or getting cold feet, or anything. We were being irrational before, and she realized it. And now…this.

I never should have tried to seek her out. That moment I first saw her, I should have just kept walking. Everything would have been much easier that way.

And yet… I can't bring myself to regret it. Not a single minute. I am so glad I saw her again. So glad for that one last look at the Sun.

So, if this is Stage Four, I wonder what I'll do at Stage Five. Will I go after her? Will I end up in some back room with security guards breathing down my neck? Will I sit in this airport for the rest of my life, wasting away, pretending none of this ever happened?

No.

I'm not going to do any of those things. There will be no Stage Five. Stage Five is something the old Mouse would have done. This whole ordeal has been me realizing, through Sunshine, how very unlike the old Mouse I am now. During Stage Five, after I broke up with Sunshine, I kept thinking of how sad she would be about what I was doing. Or, rather, not doing. I didn't get out of bed unless absolutely necessary, my grades were slipping, and I ended up in the principal's office on more than one occasion. Nobody could get through to me.

I guess, I eventually was able to stuff it all down after my dad slapped me so hard it left a mark for days and said that if I ended up in detention again, I'd get worse than a bruise. He'd never hit me before, so I wasn't too keen on finding out what would happen if I got him angry again. So I lay low, and pushed all the thoughts—good, bad, or otherwise—about Sunshine out of my mind. I tried to at least: I think I could only push them as far as the dusty corner at the back of my head.

Anyway, that was the old me. I'm better now, and I'm not going to let whatever the old me would have done about this chance meeting with Sunshine mess that up. She'd probably kill me if I did something to myself. Or to her. So I'm not going to.

This is all over. I am going to go home, and everything will be different. I'm going to try writing songs again. I'm going to do what I've always been afraid to do. For me.

I unlock the stall, splash some cold water on my face, and leave the bathroom, walking out among the masses. I see a clock on the wall: It's four minutes past noon.

I look out the window soon enough that I see a plane taking off. It's hers, it has to be. I watch it until I can't see it anymore. And when it's gone, the sun breaks out from behind the clouds, and it shines through the window, right onto me.

Chapter Thirty-two

God, his face when he left. I thought I had already seen all of his faces and smiles. I never thought I would see him be more devastated than when he found out he was moving. But I was wrong. The thing that was different about this time was that he only let his guard down for a second. His whole face fell. The light from his eyes was gone. All that brand new light, and I made it go away, so quickly. Suddenly. A candle blown out. A shot to the chest.

And then he squared his shoulders and cleared his throat. He didn't fight it. He got up, and he left. And that was it. He was gone.

I hated that he left. I didn't want it to be the end of us. I really didn't. But if I was going to do this, going home and doing the contest, I wasn't going to do it with some burden holding me back. He didn't feel like a burden yet, but he could have started to. I think I understand why he broke up with me back then. I know I do. I did the same thing to him. I am Mouse, five years ago.

I wanted to call him. I wanted him to tell me not to do the publishing competition. When something is really hard for me to do, I make others tell me to do it. It makes the doing whatever the hard thing is easier, because I'd be letting someone down if I didn't do it. Someone besides myself. I've let myself down so many times that it doesn't affect me anymore. But I hate letting other people down. So if Mouse had told me not to take the job, I wouldn't have. I'd ask him to tell me to move to Portland with him. And then I would say yes. All he had to do was tell me. I always do as I'm told.

But Mouse loves me. And I know if I told him to tell me to give it up, he wouldn't do it. Not because he's much better at disobeying than me, though he is. But because he knows how much I want this. He knows how desperately I want a book that I wrote to be in a store, on a shelf, a coffee table, a nightstand. He knows that I want my words to reach people. I want it more, or at least longer, than I have ever wanted anything. And Mouse loves me too much to ever try and take that chance away from me.

And I love him. I love all of him. I wish I'd had more time to love him. I wish I had let myself accept it sooner. Then I could have spent more time telling him. And kissing him. And holding his hand. I didn't get to hold his hand nearly enough. I didn't get to fully appreciate how wonderfully they fit with the rest of his body now that the rest of it has caught up with him.

And not enough time with my fingers in his hair. And not enough of any of it. If a whole life with him still wouldn't be enough (and it wouldn't, I know it wouldn't) then nine hours was nothing. It was the blink of an eye. Such a tiny amount of time, and so little done in it. But I love each second of those hours that I spent loving him. If blinks could be pressed in books or put in lockets, I would pick the blink that had Mouse in it and I would keep it with me forever.

I close my eyes and call the image of Mouse to mind. Him looking at me, eyes gentle, mouth soft. I feel warm. And I feel sure that I'm doing what's right. That I know what love is. And that I can trust it again.

Love doesn't tie you down. It sets you

free.

I am well loved. And so is Mouse.

Epilogue

Two Years Later

It's as beautiful as I remember. Though I don't think it's possible for any room filled with books to ever be hideous. And this isn't just one room filled with books. It's an entire building with multiple floors with multiple rooms all of them color-coded, almost all of them with stacks marching across the floor, books shelved high above my head. This is Powell's City of Books, and it will never not be beautiful.

I'm not having much in the way of a book release tour, since nobody knows or cares about me enough to come to bookstores across the country just to listen to talk about my own book. I had a release party in Chicago, and at my request, Pad & Pen got me this one signing in Portland.

In Portland, where Mouse lives. Or lived, if he's moved. I wouldn't know, I never contacted him after that day. I wanted to. But I forced myself not to. I quit him cold turkey.

I asked for Portland because (a.) this bookstore is my favorite place in the world, and (b.) because I secretly want to see Mouse again. I'm holding onto the hope that he still works there. Because then I can see him. Now that my book is finished, I'm free to work from wherever I please.

I understand seeing Mouse is probably not going to be easy. I mean, the last time I saw him, I broke his heart. (And mine. But not the point.) In the short time we were together, I walked out him multiple times, cussed him out, then landed him in the hospital (although that was more his fault than mine), confessed my love for him, had sex with him, committed to a relationship, and then changed my mind. I did all of those things, and yet, somehow managed not to say goodbye.

Why would I put either of us through remembering any of that?

Because I still love him.

Because I want him to still love me, too.

(Because cold turkey didn't work.)

Because *Retrouvailles* is published and nothing is keeping us from being in the same place anymore.

Because I'm not afraid anymore.

So I take in what I can of this beautiful place before I'm ushered upstairs to the Pearl Room so nobody will see me before the signing. I'm in a little green room, and I'm about to be left there for the next few hours before I ask the bookseller:

"Hey, do you know if a guy named Abbot Jennings works here?"

"Oh, Abbot? No, he quit about a year ago."

Damn it.

"He was nice," the girl continues. "We used to talk about weather by the coffee machine. Well, I was by the coffee machine. Abbot's more of…"

"—A tea guy," I nod. "Yeah."

She tilts her head at me, her short blonde bangs swishing against her shoulder. "Were you friends?"

"Yeah." I look down at my hands in my lap. "We were friends. Do you know what he's up to now?"

"I don't, sorry. I don't really know why he quit, either. I know that isn't very helpful."

"No, it's fine. Thank you." I smile reassuringly.

She smiles back and closes the door.

Alone in the green room, I walk a few steps into it, and fall face first onto a squashy couch. I sigh loudly and lie there for a while until I need to breathe. Getting up proves to be quite the task, my hands sinking into and between the cushions, and my body falling back each time I'm almost upright.

I'm finally sitting up, angry tears falling down my face. I should really invest in waterproof makeup. I'm glad I threw my mascara and eyeliner in my bag before I came here from my hotel.

It's the same bag from the night of Airport Purgatory. It's kind of the only one I use these days, even though there's a stain from an Americano on it. Actually, especially because there's a stain from an Americano on it. Mouse spilled his coffee onto it when he got up to toss our cups. Through his incessant apologizing, we both grabbed at a bunch of napkins to dry the stain. And our hands, as all hands in great love stories do, brushed together, and we both stayed like that a second longer than we needed to.

I don't know what I was thinking. I don't know why I just assumed Mouse would be working here still. He's moved on with his life and this is exactly what I wanted him to do. I'm really happy for him, and I hope that whatever he's doing now makes his life amazing.

It still hurts, though. So I take off my glasses and cry the rest of my makeup off my face so I can start this evening over.

He isn't here. This was the last shot I had of ever seeing him again. And it's gone.

I cry until there's nothing left, then I down an entire bottle of water to replenish all of the water I've just cried out of my system. I go to the bathroom and wash off my running makeup.

As I reapply my eyeliner, I go over the schedule for tonight in my head. I am going to talk about myself and the writing process a little bit, then read an excerpt from my book (I still haven't settled on one), and then the floor is open for questions, then I do book signing. I'm not expecting a lot of people to show up, so it shouldn't be too intimidating.

But the idea that nobody cares enough to show up? That's a little intimidating. All my life, I wanted to write so I could have a voice, so I could tell the world stories.

Jolene keeps saying it's because it's my debut, and it's only been a few weeks, and that I need to be patient. She believes in the story, which gives me hope for it.

With my makeup fixed and my face moderately presentable, I put my glasses back on and go back into the green room and flip through a copy of my book, trying to find an excerpt to read. I end up just reading it until the worker from earlier comes in and tells me that I'm being introduced in five minutes.

Grrraaah. I'll just read the first page my eyes fall on, I guess.

I spend the five minutes before I go on stretching, shaking out my nerves, and eating a brownie. My hands are clammy, so I wipe them on my jeans. They come back blue, because the jeans are new and I have yet to wash them. Perfect.

I wash them quickly, and just as I toss the paper towels in the trash, a worker calls for me.

"Ms. Ballanger? Are you ready?"

I check my face quickly, then come out of the bathroom. "Yup."

We stand in the doorway between the green room and the Pearl Room and when I hear my introduction—"It's my pleasure to introduce to you all, author Soleil Ballanger."—I put on a smile and walk out.

I'm surprised to see that there are significantly more people in attendance than I had thought there would be. In fact, in my short observation of the audience, I notice only a few empty chairs.

I step up to the podium placed at the front of the room, and the heels of my wingtip boots clack against the wooden floorboards. I look out into the audience, not really seeing faces. There's so many of them. I almost forget to speak.

"Erm—hi. Thanks so much for coming out here tonight. God, there's...a lot of you. Portland must be boring on Wednesdays."

That gets me a few laughs. My smile feels less fake. I anchor myself to the podium.

"Um…when I wrote this book, it was for a contest. Pad & Pen Publishing does this novel writing competition for all of its interns, and my boss decided my story idea was worth pursuing. It, the contest, um…starts with a plot. Then an outline, and then there's these workshops and a few tricky prompts. Not a lot of people go through with the whole thing."

I scratch my temple and sigh. "But I'd been working on this story for a while already so I kinda had a leg up. Which um. Helped."

I stop talking and it is quiet. I clear my throat.

"But I don't really think you care about that. We're here to talk about my book, not the contest during which it was written.

"I uh…I started plotting this book with a completely different frame of mind than when I started actually writing it. It was this sort of bitter story of how love can break you. And to begin with, that was all I had. It was enough to get me started, but one can only stomach so much angsty inner monologue."

I glance down at the book on the podium. "But then this thing happened that changed something in me. In the way I wanted to tell this story. So instead of it all being angst, it turned into this lengthy, painful process of Rae, the main character, coming to terms with her heartbreak, and finding out what love is, and learning that she can trust it again."

I open the book on the podium to the epigraph.

"When I was in college, I took this Ancient Literature class, and one of our required readings was The Hundred Poems of Amaru. It's just pages and pages of beautiful love poems written by King Amaru in the 7th century. My favorite out of all of them is titled *She let him in*, and I quote it in the epigraph of my book.

" 'She let him in

she did not turn away from him

there was no anger in her words

she simply looked straight at him

as though there had never been

anything between them.'

"This quote comes particularly relevant when Rae sees Jeremiah again for the first time. She stares right at him, almost through him. The pain he caused her has gone numb and seeing him again, that first time, feels like nothing to her…Which isn't really a spoiler because it's in the synopsis."

I get an idea then for which excerpt to read. I flip to Chapter 26 in the book.

"I'm going to read from Chapter 26, when Rae looks at Jeremiah, really looks at him for the first time since he came back." I push up my glasses and take a sip from a glass of water before I begin.

It was here that I realized that I was wrong about everything. Here, right here, on the kitchen floor, at three in the afternoon with lukewarm lemonade in a glass on the linoleum tiles in front of me. With Jeremiah sitting cattycornered from me, leaning against the two broken cabinet doors, his own lemonade glass rolling between his hands.

The way he looked at me: anxious and desperate, but brave. His eyes wide and his teeth tugging on his bottom lip. I was so wrong.

"Rae," he said. "You understand. Don't you understand?"

I picked up my glass and brought it halfway to my mouth. I put it back down and pulled my legs into my chest.

"Yes." Now, after all of this mess. I understand. He wanted me free. So he let me out of the trap he was so sure I was stuck in. He let me go, and he watched over me, to make sure nothing happened once I was out of the place I had gotten so comfortable in. And maybe he

should have just let me roam and figure everything out by myself, but it doesn't seem to matter half as much as it used to, now that I know all he wanted was what he thought I needed.

Jeremiah's face relaxes and he puts his glass down too, tracing the pattern on the tile instead. "Good."

I watched his fingers move. Why did he tell me that? So he would once more be in my good graces? But why would that matter now? Does he love me again? Did he ever stop?

Georgia's summer sun falls on the floor through the window right above Jeremiah's head. The light makes his mouse-brown hair shine, and it just catches onto his lashes.

And then he looks up. At me, and the light pours right into his eyes, and they're bright. And they're clear. And I see him. Not as he was. But as he is now. Now there is everything between us. And I slide across the floor to him so that will change.

I close the book and lift my head. As people clap, I let my eyes roam over the crowd. From the back, something blinding shines out at me. Like a star, but somehow more stunning. A broken star, a star gone supernova. I expect it to be gone when I blink; I must have just been seeing things. But it's still there. Constant before it shatters into nothingness.

The broken, constant star shining from the back of the room is made of brown hair flopping over onto a large forehead, with faint lines creasing it, eyebrows raised that cave in on each other, eyes that are too bright to look at, and a smile so big, it takes over all of the features and seems to shoot out and break from the face it is attached to.

It's like turning a flashlight shining in my face. It hurts, but I blink, and the light is still there.

He…Mouse. Is still there.

I turn away from the light he gives off as the applause dies down and the floor is opened for a Q&A session. I sit down at a table with the moderator and answer questions about the characters, the setting, and my writing style.

A girl in her early twenties stands up. "So in the book, Jeremiah has Type One Diabetes, and a big part of Rae's development deals with her confronting her fears and confusions about the disease, and I think she ends up in a really good place with it. You have such a good understanding of the disease, I'm just wondering if you have it yourself?"

I lean towards my microphone. "Um, I don't personally, but I know someone who does, and I know that to them it's important that a potential romantic interest has an understanding and respect for it, so that was just me trying to express the respect with which Diabetes deserves to be treated."

The girl smiles at me. "Thanks you." She sits back down.

I dart my eyes over at Mouse for a second. He winks at me.

A guy on the left side raises his hand. I call on him.

"Is it true that you're working on a French translation of your book? And if so, will it be called *Reunion* so as to mirror the French title of your book in English?"

"I am working on a French translation. It was actually my publisher's idea. My father is from France, and he raised my brother and I to speak it as a second language. But I think the title will stay the same, since it's already French. The reason I picked a French word for the title of the English version is because *retrouvailles* also has a slang definition that's sort of an adjective describing the feeling one gets when reunited with someone after being apart for a long time. And I think this meaning fits the novel particularly well. The story is about Rae's *retrouvailles* towards Jeremiah and how it changes over time."

The Q&A goes on, and all I think about

between questions is how much I want Mouse to ask me one. I want to hear his voice. I want him to know that it was him that helped me get here, and helped me write this. I want him to know that I am Rae and he is Jeremiah. That I wrote this book because I learned to trust love again.

"Okay, we're going to take one more question, and then we'll get started with the book signing," says the moderator. "Are there any other questions for Soleil?"

A few hands pop up throughout the room. Just as the moderator was about to pick someone from the left side of the room, a hand popped up in the back. I leaned over to whisper in her ear.

"Pick the one from the back."

She nods. "Um, you, in the back?"

Mouse stands up. Oh, good God. A worn-in brown sport coat. A Modest Mouse baseball t-shirt. Dark-wash jeans. He slides his hands into his jean pockets and he doesn't slouch. Mouse is all grown up. Completely; even more than he was two years ago.

"So, novel-writing isn't easy, and you talked earlier about how intense the writing competition really was. So, I guess I'm wondering what events led up to you getting the inspiration you needed to finish this book and turn it into something that has been so positively received? What was the thing that changed you?"

I look at him for a second too long before I answer. I take a steadying breath before I speak the first words I will have spoken to him in two years. Looking at him for too long proves difficult, as all I want to do is burst into tears, so I address the whole room instead.

"There was this time, two years ago, right before the actual novel-writing began, where I ran into…this person, who'd had a pretty big influence in my life. We didn't end on the best terms, so for a good bit of the time we spent together, I was trying to figure out what his reasoning was for the way he ended things with me. He really helped me understand something about love that I hadn't considered before."

"What's that?" Mouse asks.

I twist the rings on my finger. Looking down for a moment. He needs to know that I'm talking just to him. I raise my head slowly. "That love doesn't tie you down."

Mouse seems to relax. His face gets softer, and his shoulders drop.

I smile gently and continue. "It sets you free."

Book signing starts. I go sit at a table near the opposite wall. I whisper to the moderator to have the man who asked the last question to wait until everyone else's books are signed before he comes up. She relays the message to another worker, and this worker whispers to Mouse and between signings, I watch as he glances at me with a faint grin on his face.

I let the tiniest of smiles flash over my face before I beckon the first person in line over to me.

My hand starts to ache after signing my name what must be about thirty times. In the two seconds it takes for the next person to come up to the table when I wave them forward, I make a rough estimate that there's about thirty more. I shake out my hand and sign another book.

My heart beat takes over my body, my hands are quivering and clammy, and I can't stop bouncing my leg. My signature is getting sloppy. I look up after signing another book, and with a pang of anxiety, I find that there are only five more people between me and Mouse. Five smiles for strangers, five books, five thanks yous.

I sign them with the neatest handwriting I can muster. My mind is so full with the thought of Mouse that I almost write his name in the fifth book instead of the name Nadia.

And then he's in front of me. About ten feet away, waiting for me to wave him over. But right now, all I can manage to do is stare at him. He stares back, clutching a copy of my book in his hands. He's not smiling, and neither am I. I'm terrified. I have a feeling that this emotion applies to Mouse as well.

He takes the tiniest step forward and raises his brows at me. I nod microscopically, and he slowly walks the rest of the way toward me.

"Hello, Sunshine," he says in French, with an excellent accent, and a tone that sounds like he's been waiting his entire life to say those words.

"*Bonjour.*"

He keeps speaking French. "You're different."

I am. I've cut my hair since I saw him last, and I have new glasses. And I'm a novelist. I look him up and down. He's wearing brown Chelsea boots with his dark-wash jeans.

"So are you. Would you like me to sign your book?"

"Yes, but first, if I may, a few questions."

"You may."

"So, when I read this book, I couldn't help but notice many similarities between the character Rae and yourself."

"Insightful of you."

"I also found many similarities between Jeremiah and I."

I fold my hands on the tabletop. "Did you?"

"I did. And your dedication?"

"What about it?"

"It says," Mouse flips open his book. "And I quote: 'To my Jeremiah, for loving me well'."

"You are correct. And what might your question be?"

"My question, Ms. Ballanger, is this: Who is this Jeremiah to whom you refer?

"Well, I got the name from one of the members of the band Modest Mouse. Modest Mouse is a band that my Jeremiah liked, and I even used to call him Modest Mouse sometimes, as it was a play on his name, Mouse."

Mouse raised his eyebrows in mock surprise, "Why, that's my name!"

"Is it, now?"

"Yes, it says so on this Post-It." Mouse flipped to the title page, where there was a Post-It note that simply read "to Mouse".

"You're right, it does."

Mouse handed me the book. "Would you sign this for me?"

I take the book and pick up my Sharpie. "I have a question for you, actually."

"What?"

I write on the title page of the book before I look up at him and ask, "Do you still love me?"

Mouse frowns. "Sunshine, that's ridiculous. It's been almost two years since we talked. Like I said, you're so different now. And…obviously I'm different. How could I love someone I know almost nothing about now?"

I can feel myself break. I open my mouth, and my words come out weak and quiet. "I…I'm not that different, Mouse."

Mouse's face stretched into a smile in a split second. "No, I know that. I was just screwing with you."

I gasp, pretending to be angry, although I am infinitely relieved. "You asshole!"

"So, you still love me, I take it?"

"I'm not giving you this book back." I say, sliding it closer to me.

"No, no, I need it!"

"I don't believe such a cocky person deserves this book."

"I'm sorry for being an asshole,

Sunshine."

"So, this is the new Mouse, huh?"

"No! No. It's still me. I'm still Mouse."

"No, I know that." I hand him the book. "I was just screwing with you."

Mouse takes the book. "So do you love me, or don't you?"

"Do you want me to love you?"

"That's not relevant."

I raise my eyebrows.

He shift his weight back and forth on his feet. "But yes. I do. Of course I still love you. I said that I always would, and I meant it, and I really think you've grown, and I'm really proud of you for getting to this point…"

I interrupt him. "Open the book, Mouse."

He obeys, flipping it to where I signed. "'To Mouse: I was so wrong. Love love love,

Sunshine'."

"Does that answer your question?"

"Yeah," Mouse whispers to the book. "It does."

"Good."

He looks down at me. Like being felt. "So, what are your plans after this?"

"I don't have any."

"Would you like some?"

"What did you have in mind?"

"Coffee. Wandering around downtown. Portland is pretty nice at Christmastime. We could…maybe go back to my place," he offers.

"Do you still live with your roommates?"

"Oh, no. I moved out a while ago. After my songwriting career picked up, I got an apartment to myself."

My eyes go wide. "You have a

songwriting career?"

He nods once. "And an apartment to myself."

I let myself smile. "So, coffee and downtown meandering?"

"If you don't have plans."

"I don't. I just have to do a few things first. I'll meet you outside in fifteen minutes?"

"I'll be there."

After getting my stuff and thanking the staff, I go out the front doors of the bookstore, and find Mouse leaning against a bike rack, sheltered from the snow that is falling by the overhang of the building. He is reading my book. Or rather, staring at my signature on the title page.

"Hey," I say,

He stands up and snaps the book shut. "Hi. Ready to go?"

"Yeah."

He holds out his hand, and I take it, putting my other hand in the crook of his arm. We walk out into the snow and down Burnside Street.

"So you write songs?"

"Yes. And sell them. For the most part, they've only been picked up by some local indie bands. But it's going pretty well. Well enough for me to eat and live someplace alone."

"That's good."

"Although my apartment is very sparsely furnished."

"Are you happy?"

He looks over at me, smiles. "I *am* happy. Really happy."

"I'm glad."

"So, are you still living in Chicago?"

I inhale cold air. "I am. For now."

"For now?"

"I was…actually thinking about moving here. To Portland."

Mouse stops walking and gapes at me.

"Would that be weird?"

He blinks, and there is a beat of silence before he answers. "Weird? No! No, it wouldn't be weird."

"That's good."

"What would you do here?"

"I would write. I have to translate my book. If I moved here, we could date without the issues of long-distance. And I could come to my favorite bookstore whenever I want."

He lets go of my hand and stands in front of me. "You know what else you could do?"

"What?"

"You could…" he licks his lips nervously.

"Move in with me? Help me with the whole lack-of-furniture problem? Would that be weird?"

I shake my head. "No. No, it would be…amazing, actually."

Mouse gives me a blue ribbon grin. He takes my hands in his. "So we're gonna do this? Really do this?"

I nod, and kiss his grin from his mouth. I settle my forehead against his, and whisper, "Mouse and Sunshine. 'Til the end of time."

Acknowledgements

Thanks to the month of November for giving me no excuse not to write this book. Thank you, my first semester in college for not being to academically stressful in the month of November, thus allowing me the time to write this book. Thanks Kayla, Lydia, and Jazmyne for telling me to write when I didn't want to. Or at least for keeping my company and listening to my random mumbles about how terrible my writing is. Extra big thanks for Kayla, my life ring, letting her borrow her laptop so I could write this thing because mine decided to quit on me one day into the month. Thank you to all the authors whose work I have read and loved. I wouldn't be writing if I didn't want someone to love my work the way I love yours.

And finally, thank you, Caleb. For being my mighty, modest Mouse. For filling me with enough confusion, happiness, sadness, and love to write somewhat intelligently about long-distance relationships. I love you, my huckleberry friend.

Made in the USA
Charleston, SC
30 June 2015